MICHAEL'S CRAG

GRANT ALLEN

Michael's Crag

Grant Allen

© 1st World Library – Literary Society, 2004
PO Box 2211
Fairfield, IA 52556
www.1stworldlibrary.org
First Edition

LCCN: 2005906489

Softcover ISBN: 1-4218-1545-1
Hardcover ISBN: 1-4218-1445-5
eBook ISBN: 1-4218-1645-8

Purchase *"Michael's Crag"*
as a traditional bound book at:
www.1stWorldLibrary.org/purchase.asp?ISBN=1-4218-1545-1

1st World Library Literary Society is a nonprofit
organization dedicated to promoting literacy by:

- Creating a free internet library accessible from any computer worldwide.
- Hosting writing competitions and offering book publishing scholarships.

Michael's Crag
contributed by Tim, Ed & Rodney
in support of
1st World Library Literary Society

CONTENTS

CHAPTER I

A CORNISH LANDLORD

"Then you don't care for the place yourself, Tyrrel?" Eustace Le Neve said, musingly, as he gazed in front of him with a comprehensive glance at the long gray moor and the wide expanse of black and stormy water.

"It's bleak, of course; bleak and cold, I grant you; all this upland plateau about the Lizard promontory seems bleak and cold everywhere; but to my mind it has a certain wild and weird picturesqueness of its own for all that. It aims at gloominess. I confess in its own way I don't dislike it."

"For my part," Tyrrel answered, clinching his hand hard as he spoke, and knitting his brow despondently, "I simply hate it. If I wasn't the landlord here, to be perfectly frank with you, I'd never come near Penmorgan. I do it for conscience' sake, to be among my own people. That's my only reason. I disapprove of absenteeism; and now the land's mine, why, I must put up with it, I suppose, and live upon it in spite of myself. But I do it against the grain. The whole place, if I tell you the truth, is simply detestable to me."

He leaned on his stick as he spoke, and looked down gloomily at the heather. A handsome young man, Walter Tyrrel, of the true Cornish type - tall, dark, poetical-looking, with pensive eyes and a thick black mustache, which gave dignity and character to his otherwise almost too delicately feminine features. And he stood on the open moor just a hundred yards outside his own front door at Penmorgan, on the Lizard peninsula, looking westward down a great wedge-shaped gap in the solid serpentine rock to a broad belt of sea beyond without a ship or a sail on it. The view was indeed, as Eustace Le Neve admitted, a somewhat bleak and dreary one. For miles, as far as the eye could reach, on either side, nothing was to be seen but one vast heather-clad upland, just varied at the dip by bare ledges of dark rock and a single gray glimpse of tossing sea between them. A little farther on, to be sure, winding round the cliff path, one could open up a glorious prospect on either hand over the rocky islets of Kynance and Mullion Cove, with Mounts Bay and Penzance and the Land's End in the distance. That was a magnificent site - if only his ancestors had had the sense to see it. But Penmorgan House, like most other Cornish landlords' houses, had been carefully placed - for shelter's sake, no doubt - in a seaward hollow where the view was most restricted; and the outlook one got from it, over black moor and blacker rocks, was certainly by no means of a cheerful character. Eustace Le Neve himself, most cheery and sanguine of men, just home from his South American railway-laying, and with the luxuriant vegetation of the Argentine still fresh in his mind, was forced to admit, as he looked about him, that the position of his friend's house on that rolling brown moor was far from a smiling one.

"You used to come here when you were a boy, though," he objected, after a pause, with a glance at the great breakers that curled in upon the cove; "and you must surely have found it pleasant enough then, what with the bathing and the fishing and the shooting and the boating, and all the delights of the sea and the country."

Walter Tyrrel nodded his head. It was clear the subject was extremely distasteful to him.

"Yes - till I was twelve or thirteen," he said, slowly, as one who grudges assent, "in my uncle's time, I liked it well enough, no doubt. Boys don't realize the full terror of sea or cliff, you know, and are perfectly happy swimming and climbing. I used to be amphibious in those days, like a seal or an otter - in the water half my time; and I scrambled over the rocks - great heavens, it makes me giddy now just to THINK where I scrambled. But when I was about thirteen years old" - his face grew graver still - "a change seemed to come over me, and I began. . . well, I began to hate Penmorgan. I've hated it ever since. I shall always hate it. I learned what it all meant, I suppose - rocks, wrecks, and accidents. I saw how dull and gloomy it was, and I couldn't bear coming down here. I came as seldom as I dared, till my uncle died last year and left it to me. And then there was no help for it. I HAD to come down. It's a landlord's business, I consider, to live among his tenants and look after the welfare of the soil, committed to his charge by his queen and country. He holds it in trust, strictly speaking, for the nation. So I felt I must come and live here. But I hate it, all the same. I hate it! I hate it!"

He said it so energetically, and with such strange earnestness in his voice, that Eustace Le Neve, scanning his face as he spoke, felt sure there must be some good reason for his friend's dislike of his ancestral home, and forebore (like a man) to question him further. Perhaps, he thought, it was connected in Tyrrel's mind with some painful memory, some episode in his history he would gladly forget; though, to be sure, when one comes to think of it, at thirteen such episodes are rare and improbable. A man doesn't, as a rule, get crossed in love at that early age; nor does he generally form lasting and abiding antipathies. And indeed, for the matter of that, Penmorgan was quite gloomy enough in itself, in all conscience, to account for his dislike - a lonely and gaunt-looking granite-built house, standing bare and square on the edge of a black moor, under shelter of a rocky dip, in a treeless country. It must have been a terrible change for a bachelor about town, like Walter Tyrrel, to come down at twenty-eight from his luxurious club and his snug chambers in St. James' to the isolation and desolation of that wild Cornish manor-house. But the Tyrrels, he knew, were all built like that; Le Neve had been with three of the family at Rugby; and conscience was their stumbling-block.

When once a Tyrrel was convinced his duty lay anywhere, no consideration on earth would keep him from doing it.

"Let's take a stroll down by the shore," Le Neve suggested, carelessly, after a short pause, slipping his arm through his friend's.

"Your cliffs, at least, must be fine; they look grand and massive; and after three years of broiling on a South American line, this fresh sou'wester's just the thing, to my mind, to blow the cobwebs out of one."

He was a breezy-looking young man, this new-comer from beyond the sea - a son of the Vikings, Tyrrel's contemporary in age, but very unlike him in form and features; for Eustace Le Neve was fair and big-built, a florid young giant, with tawny beard, mustache, and whiskers, which he cut in a becoming Vandyke point of artistic carelessness. There was more of the artist than of the engineer, indeed, about his frank and engaging English face - a face which made one like him as soon as one looked at him. It was impossible to do otherwise. Exuberant vitality was the keynote of the man's being. And he was candidly open, too. He impressed one at first sight, by some nameless instinct, with a certain well-founded friendly confidence. A lovable soul, if ever there was one, equally liked at once by men and women.

"Our cliffs are fine," Walter Tyrrel answered, grudgingly, in the tone of one who, against his will, admits an adverse point he sees no chance of gainsaying. "They're black, and repellant, and iron-bound, and dangerous, but they're certainly magnificent. I don't deny it. Come and see them, by all means. They're the only lions we have to show a stranger in this part of Cornwall, so you'd better make the most of them."

And he took, as if mechanically, the winding path that led down the gap toward the frowning cove in the wall of cliff before them.

Grant Allen

Eustace Le Neve was a little surprised at this unexpected course, for he himself would naturally have made rather for the top of the promontory, whence they were certain to obtain a much finer and more extensive view; but he had only arrived at Penmorgan the evening before, so he bowed at once to his companion's more mature experience of Cornish scenery. They threaded their way through the gully, for it was little more - a great water-worn rent in the dark serpentine rocks, with the sea at its lower end - picking their path as they went along huge granite boulders or across fallen stones, till they reached a small beach of firm white sand, on whose even floor the waves were rolling in and curling over magnificently. It was a curious place, Eustace thought, rather dreary than beautiful. On either side rose black cliffs, towering sheer into the air, and shutting out overhead all but a narrow cleft of murky sky. Around, the sea dashed itself in angry white foam against broken stacks and tiny weed-clad skerries. At the end of the first point a solitary islet, just separated from the mainland by a channel of seething water, jutted above into the waves, with hanging tresses of blue and yellow seaweed. Tyrrel pointed to it with one hand. "That's Michael's Crag," he said, laconically. "You've seen it before, no doubt, in half a dozen pictures. It's shaped exactly like St. Michael's Mount in miniature. A marine painter fellow down here's forever taking its portrait."

Le Neve gazed around him with a certain slight shudder of unspoken disapprobation. This place didn't suit his sunny nature. It was even blacker and more dismal than the brown moorland above it. Tyrrel caught the dissatisfaction in his companion's eye before Le Neve had time to frame it in words.

"Well, you don't think much of it?" he said, inquiringly.

"I can't say I do," Le Neve answered, with apologetic frankness. "I suppose South America has spoilt me for this sort of thing. But it's not to my taste. I call it gloomy, without being even impressive."

"Gloomy," Tyrrel answered; "oh, yes, gloomy, certainly. But

impressive; well, yes. For myself, I think so. To me, it's all terribly, unspeakably, ineffably impressive. I come here every day, and sit close on the sands, and look out upon the sea by the edge of the breakers. It's the only place on this awful coast one feels perfectly safe in. You can't tumble over here, or...roll anything down to do harm to anybody."

A steep cliff path led up the sheer face of the rock to southward. It was a difficult path, a mere foothold on the ledges; but its difficulty at once attracted the engineer's attention. "Let's go up that way!" he said, waving his hand toward it carelessly. "The view from on top there must be infinitely finer."

"I believe it is," Tyrrel replied, in an unconcerned voice, like one who retails vague hearsay evidence. "I haven't seen it myself since I was a boy of thirteen. I never go along the top of the cliffs on any account."

Le Neve gazed down on him, astonished. "You BELIEVE it is!" he exclaimed, unable to conceal his surprise and wonder. "You never go up there! Why, Walter, how odd of you! I was reading up the Guidebook this morning before breakfast, and it says the walk from this point on the Penmorgan estate to Kynance Cove is the most magnificent bit of wild cliff scenery anywhere in Cornwall."

"So I'm told," Tyrrel answered, unmoved. "And I remember, as a boy, I thought it very fine. But that was long since. I never go by it."

"Why not?" Le Neve cried.

Tyrrel shrugged his shoulders and shook himself impatiently. "I don't know." he answered, in a testy sort of voice. "I don't like the cliff top... It's so dangerous, don't you know? So unsafe. So unstable. The rocks go off so sheer, and stones topple over so easily."

Le Neve laughed a little laugh of half-disguised contempt. He was moving over toward the path up the cliff side as they spoke. "Why, you used to be a first-class climber at school," he said, attempting it, "especially when you were a little chap. I remember you could scramble up trees like a monkey. What fun we had once in the doctor's orchard! And as to the cliffs, you needn't go so near you have to tumble over them. It seems ridiculous for a landowner not to know a bit of scenery on his own estate that's celebrated and talked about all over England."

"I'm not afraid of tumbling over, for myself," Tyrrel answered, a little nettled by his friend's frank tone of amusement. "I don't feel myself so useful to my queen and country that I rate my own life at too high a figure. It's the people below I'm chiefly concerned about. There's always someone wandering and scrambling about these cliffs, don't you see? - fishermen, tourists, geologists. If you let a loose stone go, it may fall upon them and crush them."

The engineer looked back upon him with a somewhat puzzled expression. "Well, that's carrying conscience a point too far," he said, with one strong hand on the rock and one sure foot in the first convenient cranny. "If we're not to climb cliffs for fear of showering down stones on those who stand below, we won't dare to walk or ride or drive or put to sea for fear of running over or colliding against somebody. We shall have to stop all our trains and keep all our steamers in harbor. There's nothing in this world quite free from risk. We've got to take it and lump it. You know the old joke about those dangerous beds - so many people die in them. Won't you break your rule just for once, and come up on top here to see the view with me?"

Tyrrel shook his head firmly. "Not to-day," he answered, with a quiet smile. "Not by that path, at any rate. It's too risky for my taste. The stones are so loose. And it overhangs the road the quarrymen go to the cave by."

Le Neve had now made good his foothold up the first four or

five steps. "Well, you've no objection to my going, at any rate?" he said, with a wave of one hand, in his cheerful good-humor. "You don't put a veto on your friends here, do you?"

"Oh, not the least objection," Tyrrel answered, hurriedly, watching him climb, none the less, with nervous interest. "It's...it's a purely personal and individual feeling. Besides," he added, after a pause," I can stop below here, if need be, and warn the quarrymen."

"I'll be back in ten minutes," Le Neve shouted from the cliff.

"No, don't hurry," his host shouted back. "Take your own time, it's safest. Once you get to the top you'd better walk along the whole cliff path to Kynance. They tell me its splendid; the view's so wide; and you can easily get back across the moor by lunch-time. Only, mind about the edge, and whatever you do, let no stones roll over."

"All right," Le Neve made answer, clinging close to a point of rock. "I'll do no damage. It's opening out beautifully on every side now. I can see round the corner to St. Michael's Mount; and the point at the end there must be Tol-Pedn-Penwith."

CHAPTER II

TREVENNACK

It was a stiff, hot climb to the top of the cliff; but as soon as he reached it, Eustace Le Neve gazed about him, enchanted at the outlook. He was not in love with Cornwall, as far as he'd seen it yet; and to say the truth, except in a few broken seaward glens, that high and barren inland plateau has little in it to attract or interest anyone, least of all a traveler fresh from the rich luxuriance of South American vegetation. But the view that burst suddenly upon Eustace Le Neve's eye as he gained the summit of that precipitous serpentine bluff fairly took his breath away. It was a rich and varied one. To the north and west loomed headland after headland, walled in by steep crags, and stretching away in purple perspective toward Marazion, St. Michael's Mount, and the Penzance district. To the south and east huge masses of fallen rock lay tossed in wild confusion over Kynance Cove and the neighboring bays, with the bare boss of the Rill and the Rearing Horse in the foreground. Le Neve stood and looked with open eyes of delight. It was the first beautiful view he had seen since he came to Cornwall; but this at least was beautiful, almost enough so to compensate for his first acute disappointment at the barrenness and gloom of the Lizard scenery.

For some minutes he could only stand with open eyes and gaze delighted at the glorious prospect. Cliffs, sea, and rocks all blended with one another in solemn harmony. Even the blackness of the great crags and the scorched air of the brown and water-logged moorland in the rear now ceased to oppress him. They fell into their proper place in one consistent and well-blended picture. But, after awhile, impelled by a desire to look down upon the next little bay beyond - for the coast is indented with endless coves and headlands - the engineer walked on along the top by a coastguard's path that threaded its way, marked by whitened stones, round the points and gullies. As he did so, he happened to notice on the very crest of the ridge that overlooked the rock they called St. Michael's Crag a tall figure of a man silhouetted in dark outline against the pale gray skyline. From the very first moment Eustace Le Neve set eyes upon that striking figure this man exerted upon him some nameless attraction. Even at this distance the engineer could see he had a certain indefinite air of dignity and distinction; and he poised himself lightly on the very edge of the cliff in a way that would no doubt have made Walter Tyrrel shudder with fear and alarm. Yet there was something about that poise quite unearthly and uncanny; the man stood so airily on his high rocky perch that he reminded Le Neve at once of nothing so much as of Giovanni da Bologna's Mercury in the Bargello at Florence; he seemed to spurn the earth as if about to spring from it with a bound; his feet were as if freed from the common bond of gravity.

It was a figure that belonged naturally to the Cornish moorland.

Le Neve advanced along the path till he nearly reached the summit where the man was standing. The point itself was a rugged tor, or little group of bare and weather-worn rocks, overlooking the sea and St. Michael's Crag below it. As the engineer drew near he saw the stranger was not alone. Under shelter of the rocks a girl lay stretched at length on a loose camel's-hair rug; her head was hatless; in her hand she held, half open, a volume of poetry. She looked up as Eustace passed, and he noted at a glance that she was dark and pretty. The Cornish type once more; bright black eyes, glossy brown hair, a rich complexion, a soft and rounded beauty.

"Cleer," the father said, warningly, in a modulated voice, as the young man approached, "don't let your hat blow away, dear; it's close by the path there."

The girl he called Cleer darted forward and picked it up, with a little blush of confusion. Eustace Le Neve raised his hat, by way of excuse for disturbing her, and was about to pass on, but the view down into the bay below, with the jagged and pointed crag islanded in white foam, held him spellbound for a moment. He paused and gazed at it. "This is a lovely lookout, sir," he said, after a second's silence, as if to apologize for his intrusion, turning round to the stranger, who still stood poised like a statue on the natural pedestal of lichen-covered rock beside him. "A lovely lookout and a wonderful bit of wild coast scenery."

"Yes," the stranger answered, in a voice as full of dignity as his presence and his mien. "It's the grandest spot along the Cornish coast. From here you can see in one view St. Michael's Mount, St. Michael's Crag, St. Michael's Church, and St. Michael's Promontory. The whole of this country, indeed, just teems with St. Michael."

"Which is St. Michael's Promontory?" the young man asked, with a side glance at Cleer, as they called the daughter. He wasn't sorry indeed for the chance of having a second look at her.

"Why Land's End, of course," the dignified stranger answered at once, descending from his perch as he spoke, with a light spring more like a boy's than a mature man's. "You must surely know those famous lines in 'Lycidas' about

'The fable of Bellerus old,
Where the Great Vision of the guarded mount
Looks towards Namancos and Bayona's hold;
ook homeward, angel, now, and melt with ruth.'"

"Yes, I KNOW them, of course," Eustace answered with

ingenuous shyness; "but as so often happens with poetry, to say the truth, I'm afraid I attached no very definite idea to them. The music so easily obscures the sense; though the moment you suggest it, I see they can't possibly mean anyone but St. Michael."

"My father's very much interested in the antiquities of Cornwall," the girl Cleer put in, looking up at him somewhat timidly; "so he naturally knows all these things, and perhaps he expects others to know them unreasonably."

"We've every ground for knowing them," the father went on, glancing down at her with tender affection. "We're Cornish to the backbone - Cornish born and bred, if ever there were Cornishmen. Every man of my ancestors was a Tre, Pol, or Pen, to the tenth generation backward; and I'm descended from the Bassets, too - the Bassets of Tehidy. You must have heard of the Bassets in Cornish history. They owned St. Michael's Mount before these new-fangled St. Aubyn people."

"It's Lord St. Levan's now, isn't it?" Le Neve put in, anxious to show off his knowledge of the local aristocracy.

"Yes, they've made him Lord St. Levan," the dignified stranger answered, with an almost imperceptible curl of his delicate lower lip. "They've made him Lord St. Levan. The queen can make one anything. He was plain Sir John St. Aubyn before that, you know; his family bought the Mount from my ancestors - the Bassets of Tehidy. They're new people at Marazion - new people altogether. They've only been there since 1660."

Le Neve smiled a quiet smile. That seemed to him in his innocence a fairly decent antiquity as things go nowadays. But the dignified stranger appeared to think so little of it that his new acquaintance abstained from making note or comment on it. He waited half a moment to see whether Cleer would speak again; he wanted to hear that pleasant voice once more; but as she held her peace, he merely raised his hat, and accepting the dismissal, continued his walk round the cliffs alone. Yet, somehow, the rest of the way, the figure of that statuesque stranger haunted him. He looked back once or twice. The descendant of the Bassets of Tehidy had now resumed his high pedestal upon the airy tor, and was gazing away seaward, like the mystic Great Vision of his own Miltonic quotation, toward the Spanish coast, wrapped round in a loose cloak of most poetic dimensions. Le Neve wondered who he was, and what errand could have brought him there.

At the point called the Rill, he diverged from the path a bit, to get that beautiful glimpse down into the rock-strewn cove and smooth white sands at Kynance. A coastguard with brush and pail was busy as he passed by renewing the whitewash on the landmark boulders that point the path on dark nights to the stumbling wayfarer. Le Neve paused and spoke to him. "That's a fine-looking man, my friend, the gentleman on the tor there," he said, after a few commonplaces. "Do you happen to know his name? Is he spending the summer about here?"

The man stopped in his work and looked up. His eye lighted with pleasure on the dignified stranger. "Yes; he's one of the right sort, sir," he answered, with a sort of proprietary pride in the distinguished figure. "A real old Cornish gentleman of the good old days, he is, if ever you see one. That's Trevennack of Trevennack; and Miss Cleer's his daughter. Fine old crusted Cornish names, every one of them; I'm a Cornishman myself, and I know them well, the whole grand lot of them. The Trevennacks and the Bassets, they was all one, time gone by; they owned St. Michael's Mount, and Penzance, and Marazion, and Mullion here. They owned Penmorgan, too, afore the Tyrrels bought it up. Michael Basset Trevennack, that's the gentleman's full name; the eldest son of the eldest son is always a Michael, to keep up the memory of the times gone by, when they was Guardians of the Mount and St. Michael's Constables. And the lady's Miss Cleer, after St. Cleer of Cornwall - her that gives her name still to St. Cleer by Liskeard."

"And do they live here?" Le Neve asked, much interested in the intelligent local tone of the man's conversation.

"Lord bless you, no, sir. They don't live nowhere. They're in the service, don't you see. They lives in Malta or Gibraltar, or wherever the Admiralty sends him. He's an Admiralty man, he is, connected with the Vittling Yard. I was in the navy myself, on the good old Billy Ruffun, afore I was put in the Coastguards, and I knowed him well when we was both together on the Mediterranean Station. Always the same grand old Cornish gentleman, with them gracious manners, so haughty like, an' yet so condescending, wherever they put him. A gentleman born. No gentleman on earth more THE gentleman all round than Trevennack of Trevennack."

"Then he's staying down here on a visit?" Le Neve went on, curiously, peering over the edge of the cliffs, as he spoke, to observe the cormorants.

"Don't you go too nigh, sir," the coastguard put in, warningly. "She's slippery just there. Yes, they're staying down in Oliver's lodgings at Gunwalloe. He's on leave, that's where it is. Every three or four years he gets leave from the Vittling and comes home to England; and then he always ups and runs down to the Lizard, and wanders about on the cliffs by himself like this, with Miss Cleer to keep him company. He's a chip of the old rock, he is - Cornish granite to the core, as the saying goes; and he can't be happy away from it. You'll see him any day standing like that on the very edge of the cliff, looking across over the water, as if he was a coastguard hisself, and always sort o' perched on the highest bit of rock he can come nigh anywhere."

"He looks an able man," Le Neve went on, still regarding the stranger, poised now as before on the very summit of the tor, with his cloak wrapped around him.

"Able? I believe you! Why, he's the very heart and soul, the brains and senses of the Vittling Department. The navy'd starve if it wasn't for him. He's a Companion of St. Michael and St. George, Mr. Trevennack is. 'Tain't every one as is a Companion of St. Michael and St. George. The queen made him that herself for his management of the Vittling." "It's a strange place for a man in his position to spend his holiday," Le Neve went on, reflectively. "You'd think, coming back so seldom, he'd want to see something of London, Brighton, Scarborough, Scotland."

The coastguard looked up, and held his brush idle in one hand with a mysterious air. "Not when you come to know his history," he answered, gazing hard at him.

"Oh, there's a history to him, is there?" Le Neve answered, not surprised. "Well, he certainly has the look of it."

The coastguard nodded his head and dropped his voice still lower. "Yes, there's a history to him," he replied. "And that's why you'll always see Trevennack of Trevennack on the top of the cliff, and never at the bottom. - Thank'ee very kindly, sir; it ain't often we gets a chance of a good cigar at Kynance. - Well, it must be fifteen year now - or maybe sixteen - I don't mind the right time - Trevennack came down in old Squire Tyrrel's days, him as is buried at Mullion Church town, and stopped at Gunwalloe, same as he might be stopping there in his lodgings nowadays. He had his only son with him, too, a fine-looking young gentleman, they say, for his age, for I wasn't here then - I was serving my time under Admiral De Horsey on the good old Billy Ruffun - the very picture of Miss Cleer, and twelve year old or thereabouts; and they called him Master Michael, the same as they always call the eldest boy of the Trevennacks of Trevennack. Aye, and one day they two, father and son, were a-strolling on the beach under the cliffs by Penmorgan - mind them stones on the edge, sir; they're powerful loose - don't you drop none over - when, just as you might loosen them pebbles there with your foot, over came a shower o' small bits from the cliff on top, and as sure as you're livin', hit the two on 'em right so, sir. Mr. Trevennack himself, he wasn't much hurt - just bruised a bit on the forehead, for he was wearing a Scotch cap; but Master Michael, well, it caught him right on the top of the head, and afore they knowed what it was, it smashed his skull in. Aye, that it did, sir, just so; it smashed the boy's skull in. They carried him home, and cut the bone out, and trepanned him; but bless you, it wa'n't no good; he lingered on for a night, and then, afore morning, he died, insensible."

"What a terrible story!" Le Neve exclaimed, with a face of horror, recoiling instinctively from the edge of the cliff that had wrought this evil. "Aye, you may well say so. It was rough on him," the coastguard went on, with the calm criticism of his kind. "His only son - and all in a minute like, as you may term it - such a promising young gentleman! It was rough, terrible rough on him. So from that day to this, whenever Trevennack has a holiday, down he comes here to Gunwalloe, and walks about the cliffs, and looks across upon the rocks by Penmorgan Point, or stands on the top of Michael's Crag, just over against the spot where his boy was hurted. An' he never wants to go nowhere else in all England, but just to stand like that on the very edge of the cliff, and look over from atop, and brood, and think about it."

As the man spoke, it flashed across Le Neve's mind at once that Trevennack's voice had quivered with a strange thrill of emotion as he uttered that line, no doubt pregnant with meaning for him. "Look homeward, Angel, now, and melt with ruth." He was thinking of his own boy, most likely, not of the poet's feigned Lycidas.

"He'll stand like that for hours," the coastguard went on confidentially, "musing like to himself, with Miss Cleer by his side, reading in her book or doing her knitting or something. But you couldn't get him, for love or money, to go BELOW the cliffs, no, not if you was to kill him. He's AFRAID of going below - that's where it is; he always thinks something's sure to tumble from the top on him. Natural enough, too, after all that's been. He likes to get as high as ever he can in the air, where he can see all around him, and be certain there ain't

Grant Allen

anyone above to let anything drop as might hurt him. Michael's Crag's where he likes best to stand, on the top there by the Horse; he always chooses them spots. In Malta it was San Mickayly; and in Gibraltar it was the summit of Europa Point, by the edge of the Twelve Apostles' battery."

"How curious!" Le Neve exclaimed. "It's just the other way on now, with my friend Mr. Tyrrel. I'm stopping at Penmorgan, but Mr. Tyrrel won't go on TOP of the cliffs for anything. He says he's afraid he might let something drop by accident on the people below him."

The coastguard grew suddenly graver. "Like enough," he said, stroking his chin. "Like enough; and right, too, for him, sir. You see, he's a Tyrrel, and he's bound to be cautious.'

"Why so?" Le Neve asked, somewhat puzzled. "Why a Tyrrel more than the rest of us?"

The man hesitated and stared hard at him.

"Well, it's like this, sir," he answered at last, with the shame-faced air of the intelligent laboring man who confesses to a superstition. "We Cornish are old-fashioned, and we has our ideas. The Tyrrels are new people like, in Cornwall, as we say; they came in only with Cromwell's folk, when he fought the Grenvilles; but it's well beknown in the county bad luck goes with them. You see, they're descended from that Sir Walter Tyrrel you'll read about in the history books, him as killed King William Rufious in the New Forest. You'll hear all about it at Rufious' Stone, where the king was killed; Sir Walter, he drew, and he aimed at a deer, and the king was standing by; and the bullet, it glanced aside - or maybe it was afore bullets, and then it'd be an arrow; but anyhow, one or t'other, it hit the king, and he fell, and died there. The stone's standing to this day on the place where he fell, and I've seen it, and read of it when I was in hospital at Netley. But Sir Walter, he got clear away, and ran across to France; and ever since that time they've called the eldest son of the Tyrrels Walter, same as they've called the eldest son of the Trevennacks Michael. But they say every Walter Tyrrel that's born into the world is bound, sooner or later, to kill his man unintentional. So he do right to avoid going too near the cliffs, I say. We shouldn't tempt Providence. And the Tyrrels is all a conscientious people."

Grant Allen

CHAPTER III

FACE TO FACE

When Eustace Le Neve returned to lunch at Penmorgan that day he was silent to his host about Trevennack of Trevennack. To say the truth, he was so much attracted by Miss Cleer's appearance that he didn't feel inclined to mention having met her. But he wanted to meet her again for all that, and hoped he would do so. Perhaps Tyrrel might know the family, and ask them round to dine some night. At any rate, society is rare at the Lizard. Sooner or later, he felt sure, he'd knock up against the mysterious stranger somewhere. And that involved the probability of knocking up against the mysterious stranger's beautiful daughter.

Next morning after breakfast, however, he made a vigorous effort to induce Walter Tyrrel to mount the cliff and look at the view from Penmorgan Point toward the Rill and Kynance. It was absurd, he said truly, for the proprietor of such an estate never to have seen the most beautiful spot in it. But Tyrrel was obdurate. On the point of actually mounting the cliff itself he wouldn't yield one jot or tittle. Only, after much persuasion, he consented at last to cross the headland by the fields at the back and come out at the tor above St. Michael's Crag, provided always Eustace would promise he'd neither go near the edge himself nor try to induce his friend to approach it.

Satisfied with this lame compromise - for he really wished his host to enjoy that glorious view - Eustace Le Neve turned up the valley behind the house, with Walter Tyrrel by his side, and after traversing several fields, through gaps in the stone walls, led out his companion at last to the tor on the headland.

As they approached it from behind, the engineer observed, not without a faint thrill of pleasure, that Trevennack's stately figure stood upright as before upon the wind-swept pile of fissured rocks, and that Cleer sat reading under its shelter to leeward. But by her side this morning sat also an elder lady, whom Eustace instinctively recognized as her mother - a graceful, dignified lady, with silvery white hair and black Cornish eyes, and features not untinged by the mellowing, hallowing air of a great sorrow.

Le Neve raised his hat as they drew near, with a pleased smile of welcome, and Trevennack and his daughter both bowed in return. "A glorious morning!" the engineer said, drinking in to the full the lovely golden haze that flooded and half-obscured the Land's End district; and Trevennack assented gravely. "The crag stands up well in this sunshine against the dark water behind," he said, waving one gracious hand toward the island at his foot, and poising lighter than ever.

"Oh, take care!" Walter Tyrrel cried, looking up at him, on tenterhooks. It's so dangerous up there! You might tumble any minute."

"*I* never tumble," Trevennack made answer with solemn gravity, spreading one hand on either side as if to balance himself like an acrobat. But he descended as he spoke and took his place beside them.

Tyrrel looked at the view and looked at the pretty girl. It was evident he was quite as much struck by the one as by the other. Indeed, of the two, Cleer seemed to attract the larger share of his attention. For some minutes they stood and talked, all five of them together, without further introduction than their common admiration for that exquisite bay, in which Trevennack appeared to take an almost proprietary interest. It gratified him, obviously, a Cornish man, that these strangers (as he thought them) should be so favorably impressed by his native county. But Tyrrel all the while looked ill at ease, though he sidled away as far as possible from the edge of the cliff, and sat down near Cleer at a safe distance from the precipice. He was silent and preoccupied. That mattered but little, however, as the rest did all the talking, especially Trevennack, who turned out to be indeed a perfect treasure-house of Cornish antiquities and Cornish folk-lore.

"I generally stand below, on top of Michael's Crag," he said to Eustace, pointing it out, "when the tide allows it; but when it's high, as it is now, such a roaring and seething scour sets through the channel between the rock and the mainland that no swimmer could stem it; and then I come up here, and look down from above upon it. It's the finest point on all our Cornish coast, this point we stand on. It has the widest view, the purest air, the hardest rock, the highest and most fantastic tor of any of them."

"My husband's quite an enthusiast for this particular place," Mrs. Trevennack interposed, watching his face as she spoke with a certain anxious and ill-disguised wifely solicitude.

"He's come here for years. It has many associations for us."

"Some painful and some happy," Cleer added, half aloud; and Tyrrel, nodding assent, looked at her as if expecting some marked recognition.

"You should see it in the pilchard season," her father went on, turning suddenly to Eustace with much animation in his voice. "That's the time for Cornwall - a month or so later than now - you should see it then, for picturesqueness and variety. 'When the corn is in the shock,' says our Cornish rhyme, 'Then the fish are off the rock' - and the rock's St. Michael's. The HUER, as we call him, for he gives the hue and cry from the hill-top lookout when the fish are coming, he stands on Michael's Crag just below there, as I stand myself so often, and when he sights the shoals by the ripple on the water, he motions to the boats which way to go for the pilchards. Then the rowers in the lurkers, as we call our seine-boats, surround the shoal with a tuck-net, or drag the seine into Mullion Cove, all alive with a mass of shimmering silver. The jowsters come down with their carts on to the beach, and hawk them about round the neighborhood - I've seen them twelve a penny; while in the curing-houses they're bulking them and pressing them as if for dear life, to send away to Genoa, Leghorn, and Naples. That's where all our fish go - to the Catholic south. 'The Pope and the Pilchards,' says our Cornish toast; for it's the Friday fast that makes our only market."

"You can see them on St. George's Island in Looe Harbor," Cleer put in quite innocently. "They're like a sea of silver there - on St. George's Island."

"My dear," her father corrected with that grave, old-fashioned courtesy which the coast-guard had noted and described as at once so haughty and yet so condescending, "how often I've begged of you NOT to call it St. George's Island! It's St. Nicholas' and St. Michael's - one may as well be correct - and till a very recent date a chapel to St. Michael actually stood there upon the rocky top; it was only destroyed, you remember, at the time of the Reformation."

"Everybody CALLS it St. George's now," Cleer answered, with girlish persistence. And her father looked round at her sharply, with an impatient snap of the fingers, while Mrs. Trevennack's eye was fixed on him now more carefully and more earnestly, Tyrrel observed, than ever.

"I wonder why it is," Eustace Le Neve interposed, to spare Cleer's feelings, "that so many high places, tops of mountains and so forth, seem always to be dedicated to St. Michael in particular? He seems to love such airy sites. There's St. Michael's Mount here, you know, and Mont St. Michel in Normandy; and at Le Puy, in Auvergne, there's a St. Michael's Rock, and at ever so many other places I can't remember

Grant Allen

this minute."

Trevennack was in his element. The question just suited him. He smiled a curious smile of superior knowledge. "You've come to the right place for information," he said, blandly, turning round to the engineer. "I'm a Companion of St. Michael and St. George myself, and my family, as I told you, once owned St. Michael's Mount; so, for that and various other reasons, I've made a special study of St. Michael the Archangel, and all that pertains to him." And then he went on to give a long and learned disquisition, which Le Neve and Walter Tyrrel only partially followed, about the connection between St. Michael and the Celtic race, as well as about the archangel's peculiar love for high and airy situations. Most of the time, indeed, Le Neve was more concerned in watching Cleer Trevennack's eyes, as her father spoke, than in listening to the civil servant's profound dissertation. He gathered, however, from the part he caught, that St. Michael the Archangel had been from early days a very important and powerful Cornish personage, and that he clung to high places on the tors and rocks because he had to fight and subdue the Prince of the Air, whom he always destroyed at last on some pointed pinnacle. And now that he came to think of it, Eustace vaguely recollected he had always seen St. Michael, in pictures or stained glass windows, delineated just so - with drawn sword and warrior's mien - in the act of triumphing over his dragon-like enemy on the airy summit of some tall jagged crag or rock-bound precipice.

As for Mrs. Trevennack, she watched her husband every moment he spoke with a close and watchful care, which Le Neve hardly noticed, but which didn't for a minute escape Walter Tyrrel's more piercing and observant scrutiny.

At last, as the amateur lecturer was beginning to grow somewhat prolix, a cormorant below created a slight diversion for awhile by settling in his flight on the very highest point of Michael's Crag, and proceeding to preen his glittering feathers in the full golden flood of that bright August sunlight.

With irrepressible boyish instinct Le Neve took up a stone, and was just on the point of aiming it (quite without reason) at the bird on the pinnacle.

But before he could let it go, the two other men, moved as if by a single impulse, had sprung forward with a bound, and in the self-same tone and in the self-same words cried out with one accord, in a wildly excited voice, "For God's sake, don't throw! You don't know how dangerous it is!"

Le Neve let his hand drop flat, and allowed the stone to fall from it. As he did so the two others stood back a pace, as if guarding him, but kept their hands still ready to seize the engineer's arm if he made the slightest attempt at motion. Eustace felt they were watching him as one might watch a madman. For a moment they were silent. Trevennack was the first to speak. His voice had an earnest and solemn ring in it, like a reproving angel's. "How can you tell what precious life may be passing below?" he said, with stern emphasis, fixing Le Neve with his reproachful eye. "The stone might fall short. It might drop out of sight. You might kill whomsoever it struck, unseen. And then" - he drank in a deep breath, gasping - "you would know you were a murderer."

Walter Tyrrel drew himself up at the words like one stung. "No, no! not a murderer!" he cried; "not quite as bad as a murderer! It wouldn't be murder, surely. It would be accidental homicide - unintentional, unwilled - a terrible result of most culpable carelessness, of course; but it wouldn't be quite murder; don't call it murder. I can't allow that. Not that name by any means. . . .Though to the end of your life, Eustace, if you were to kill a man so, you'd never cease to regret it and mourn over it daily; you'd never cease to repent your guilty carelessness in sackcloth and ashes."

He spoke so seriously, so earnestly, with such depth of personal feeling, that Trevennack, starting back, stood and gazed at him slowly with those terrible eyes, like one who awakens by degrees from a painful dream to some awful reality. Tyrrel winced before his scrutiny. For a moment the elder man just looked at him and stared. Then he took one step forward. "Sir," he said, in a very low voice, half broken with emotion, "I had a dear son of my own once; a very dear, dear son. He was killed by such an ACCIDENT on this very spot. No wonder I remember it."

Mrs. Trevennack and Cleer both gave a start of surprise. The man's words astonished them; for never before, during fifteen long years, had that unhappy father alluded in any way in overt words to his son's tragic end. He had brooded and mused over it in his crushed and wounded spirit; he had revisited the scene of his loss whenever opportunity permitted him; he had made of his sorrow a cherished and petted daily companion; but he had stored it up deep in his own inmost heart, never uttering a word of it even to his wife or daughter. The two women knew Michael Trevennack must be profoundly moved, indeed, so to tear open the half-healed wound in his tortured bosom before two casual strangers.

But Tyrrel, too, gave a start as he spoke, and looked hard at the careworn face of that unhappy man. "Then you're Mr. Trevennack!" he exclaimed, all aghast. "Mr. Trevennack of the Admiralty!"

And the dignified stranger answered, bowing his head very low, "Yes, you've guessed me right. I'm Michael Trevennack."

With scarcely a word of reply Walter Tyrrel turned and strode away from the spot. "I must go now," he muttered faintly, looking at his watch with some feigned surprise, as a feeble excuse. "I've an appointment at home." He hadn't the courage to stay. His heart misgave him. Once fairly round the corner he fled like a wounded creature, too deeply hurt even to cry. Eustace Le Neve, raising his hat, hastened after him, all mute wonder. For several hundred yards they walked on side by side across the open heathy moor. Then, as they passed the first wall, Tyrrel paused for a moment and spoke. "NOT a murderer!" he cried in his anguish; "oh, no, not quite as bad as a murderer, surely, Eustace; but still, a culpable homicide. Oh, God, how terrible."

And even as he disappeared across the moor to eastward, Trevennack, far behind, seized his wife's arm spasmodically, and clutching it tight in his iron grip, murmured low in a voice of supreme conviction, "Do you see what that means, Lucy? I can read it all now. It was HE who rolled down that cursed stone. It was HE who killed our boy. And I can guess who he is. He must be Tyrrel of Penmorgan."

Cleer didn't hear the words. She was below, gazing after them.

CHAPTER IV

TYRREL'S REMORSE

The two young men walked back, without interchanging another word, to the gate of the manor-house. Tyrrel opened it with a swing. Then, once within his own grounds, and free from prying eyes, he sat down forthwith upon a little craggy cliff that overhung the carriage-drive, buried his face in his hands, and, to Le Neve's intense astonishment, cried long and silently. He let himself go with a rush; that's the Cornish nature. Eustace Le Neve sat by his side, not daring to speak, but in mute sympathy with his sorrow. For many minutes neither uttered a sound. At last Tyrrel looked up, and in an agony of remorse, turned round to his companion. "Of course you understand," he said.

And Eustace answered reverently, "Yes, I think I understand. Having come so near doing the same thing myself, I sympathize with you."

Tyrrel paused a moment again. His face was like marble. Then he added, in a tone of the profoundest anguish, "Till this minute, Eustace, I've never told anybody. And if it hadn't been forced out of me by that poor man's tortured and broken-hearted face, I wouldn't have told you now. But could I look at him to-day and not break down before him?"

"How did it all happen?" Le Neve asked, leaning forward and clasping his friend's arm with a brotherly gesture.

Tyrrel answered with a deep sigh, "Like this. I'll make a clean breast of it all at last. I've bottled it up too long. I'll tell you now, Eustace.

"Nearly sixteen years ago I was staying down here at Penmorgan with my uncle. The Trevennacks, as I learned afterward, were in lodgings at Gunwalloe. But, so far as I can remember at present, I never even saw them. To the best of my belief I never set eyes on Michael Trevennack himself before this very morning. If I'd known who he was, you may be pretty sure I'd have cut off my right hand before I'd allowed myself to speak to him.

"Well, one day that year I was strolling along the top of the cliff by Michael's Crag, with my uncle beside me, who owned Penmorgan. I was but a boy then, and I walked by the edge more than once, very carelessly. My uncle knew the cliffs, though, and how dangerous they were; he knew men might any time be walking below, digging launces in the sand, or getting lobworms for their lines, or hunting serpentine to polish, or looking for sea-bird's eggs among the half-way ledges. Time after time he called out to me, 'Walter, my boy, take care; don't go so near the edge, you'll tumble over presently.' And time after time I answered him back, like a boy that I was, 'Oh, I'm all right, uncle. No fear about me. I can take care of myself. These cliffs don't crumble. They're a deal too solid.'

"At last, when he saw it was no good warning me that way any longer, he turned round to me rather sharply - he was a Tyrrel, you see, and conscientious, as we all of us are - it runs in the blood somehow - 'If you don't mind for yourself, at least mind for others. Who can say who may be walking underneath those rocks? If you let a loose stone fall you may commit manslaughter.'

"I laughed, and thought ill of him. He was such a fidget! I was only a boy. I considered him absurdly and unnecessarily particular. He had stalked on a yard or two in front. I loitered

Grant Allen

behind, and out of pure boyish deviltry, as I was just above Michael's Crag, I loosened some stones with my foot and showered them over deliberately. Oh, heavens, I feel it yet; how they rattled and rumbled!

"My uncle wasn't looking. He walked on and left me behind. He didn't see me push them. He didn't see them fall. He didn't hear them rattle. But as they reached the bottom I heard myself - or thought I heard - a vague cry below. A cry as of some one wounded. I was frightened at that; I didn't dare to look down, but ran on to my uncle. Not till some hours after did I know the whole truth, for we walked along the cliffs all the way to Kynance, and then returned inland by the road to the Lizard.

"That afternoon, late, there was commotion at Penmorgan. The servants brought us word how a bit of the cliff near Michael's Crag had foundered unawares, and struck two people who were walking below - a Mr. Trevennack, in lodgings at Gunwalloe, and his boy Michael. The father wasn't much hurt, they said; but the son - oh, Eustace! the son was dangerously wounded. ... I listened in terror.... He lived out the night, and died next morning."

Tyrrel leaned back in agony as he spoke, and looked utterly crushed. It was an awful memory. Le Neve hardly knew what to say, the man's remorse was so poignant. After all those years the boy's thoughtless act seemed to weigh like a millstone round the grown man's neck. Eustace held his peace, and felt for him. By and by Tyrrel went on again, rocking himself to and fro on his rough seat as he spoke. "For fifteen years," he said, piteously, "I've borne this burden in my heart, and never told anybody. I tell it now first of all men to you. You're the only soul on earth who shares my secret."

"Then your uncle didn't suspect it?" Eustace asked, all breathless.

Walter Tyrrel shook his head. "On the contrary," he answered, "he said to me next day, 'How glad I am Walter, my boy, I called you away from the cliff that moment! It was quite providential. For if you'd loosened a stone, and then this thing had happened, we'd both of us have believed it was YOU that did it?' I was too frightened and appalled to tell him it WAS I. I thought they'd hang me. But from that day to this - Eustace, Eustace, believe me - I've never ceased to think of it! I've never forgiven myself!"

"Yet it was an accident after all," Le Neve said, trying to comfort him.

"No, no; not quite. I should have been warned in time. I should have obeyed my uncle. But what would you have? It's the luck of the Tyrrels."

He spoke plaintively. Le Neve pulled a piece of grass and began biting it to hide his confusion. How near he might have come to doing the same thing himself. He thanked his stars it wasn't he. He thanked his stars he hadn't let that stone drop from the cliff that morning.

Tyrrel was the first to break the solemn silence. "You can understand now," he said, with an impatient gesture, "why I hate Penmorgan. I've hated it ever since. I shall always hate it. It seems like a mute reminder of that awful day. In my uncle's time I never came near it. But as soon as it was my own I felt I must live upon it; and now, this terror of meeting Trevennack some day has made life one long burden to me. Sooner or later I felt sure I should run against him. They told me how he came down here from time to time to see where his son died, and I knew I should meet him. Now you can understand, too, why I hate the top of the cliffs so much, and WILL walk at the bottom. I had two good reasons for that. One I've told you already; the other was the fear of coming across Trevennack."

Le Neve turned to him compassionately. "My dear fellow," he said, "you take it too much to heart. It was so long ago, and you were only a child. The... the accident might happen to any

Grant Allen

boy any day."

"Yes, yes," Tyrrel answered, passionately. I know all that. I try, so, to console myself. But then I've wrecked that unhappy man's life for him."

"He has his daughter still," Le Neve put in, vaguely. It was all he could think of to say by way of consolation; and to him, Cleer Trevennack would have made up for anything.

A strange shade passed over Tyrrel's face. Eustace noted it instinctively. Something within seemed to move that Cornish heart. "Yes, he has his daughter still," the Squire of Penmorgan answered, with a vacant air. "But for me, that only makes things still worse than before.... How can she pardon my act? What can she ever think of me?"

Le Neve turned sharply round upon him. There was some undercurrent in the tone in which he spoke that suggested far more than the mere words themselves might perhaps have conveyed to him. "What do you mean?" he asked, all eager, in a quick, low voice. "You've met Miss Trevennack before? You've seen her? You've spoken to her?"

For a second Tyrrel hesitated; then, with a burst, he spoke out. "I may as well tell you all," he cried, "now I've told you so much. Yes, I've met her before, I've seen her, I've spoken to her."

"But she didn't seem to recognize you," Le Neve objected, taken aback.

Tyrrel shook his head despondently. "That's the worst of it all," he answered, with a very sad sigh. "She didn't even remember me.... She was so much to me; and to her - why, to HER, Eustace - I was less than nothing."

"And you knew who she was when you saw her just now?" Le Neve asked, greatly puzzled.

"Yes and no. Not exactly. I knew she was the person I'd seen and talked with, but I'd never heard her name, nor connected her in any way with Michael Trevennack. If I had, things would be different. It's a terrible Nemesis. I'll tell you how it happened. I may as well tell all. But the worst point of the whole to me in this crushing blow is to learn that that girl is Michael Trevennack's daughter."

"Where and when did you meet her then?" Le Neve asked, growing curious.

"Quite casually, once only, some time since, in a railway carnage. It must be two years ago now, and I was going from Bath to Bournemouth. She traveled with me in the same compartment as far as Temple Combe, and I talked all the way with her; I can remember every word of it....Eustace, it's foolish of me to acknowledge it, perhaps, but in those two short hours I fell madly in love with her. Her face has lived with me ever since; I've longed to meet her, But I was stupidly afraid to ask her name before she got out of the train; and I had no clue at all to her home or her relations. Yet, a thousand times since I've said to myself, 'If ever I marry I'll marry that girl who went in the carriage from Bath to Temple Combe with me.' I've cherished her memory from that day to this. You mayn't believe, I dare say, in love at first sight; but this I can swear to you was a genuine case of it."

"I can believe in it very well," Le Neve answered, most truthfully, "now I've seen Miss Trevennack."

Tyrrel looked at him, and smiled sadly. "Well, when I saw her again this morning," he went on, after a short pause, "my heart came up into my mouth. I said to myself, with a bound, 'It's she! It's she! At last I've found her.' And it dashed my best hopes to the ground at once to see she didn't even remember having met me."

Le Neve looked at him shyly. "Walter," he said, after a short struggle, "I'm not surprised you fell in love with her. And shall

I tell you why? I fell in love with her myself, too, the moment I saw her."

Tyrrel turned to him without one word of reproach. "Well, we're no rivals now," he answered, generously. "Even if she would have me - even if she loved me well - how could I ask her to take - her brother's murderer?"

Le Neve drew a long breath. He hadn't thought of that before. But had it been other wise, he couldn't help feeling that the master of Penmorgan would have been a formidable rival for a penniless engineer just home from South America.

For already Eustace Le Neve was dimly aware, in his own sanguine mind, that he meant to woo and win that beautiful Cleer Trevennack.

CHAPTER V

A STRANGE DELUSION

Trevennack and his wife sat alone that night in their bare rooms at Gunwalloe. Cleer had gone out to see some girls of her acquaintance who were lodging close by in a fisherman's house; and the husband and wife were left for a few hours by themselves together.

"Michael," Mrs. Trevennack began, as soon as they were alone, rising up from her chair and coming over toward him tenderly, "I was horribly afraid you were going to break out before those two young men on the cliff to-day. I saw you were just on the very brink of it. But you resisted bravely. Thank you so much for that. You're a dear good fellow. I was so pleased with you and so proud of you."

"Break out about our poor boy?" Trevennack asked, with a dreamy air, passing his bronzed hand wearily across his high white forehead.

His wife seated herself sideways upon the arm of his chair, and bent over him as he sat, with wifely confidence. "No, no, dear," she said, taking his hand in hers and soothing it with her soft palm. "About - YOU know - well, of course, that other thing."

At the mere hint, Trevennack leaned back and drew himself up proudly to his full height, like a soldier. He looked majestic as

Grant Allen

he sat there - every inch a St. Michael. "Well, it's hard to keep such a secret," he answered, laying his free hand on his breast, "hard to keep such a secret; and I own, when they were talking about it, I longed to tell them. But for Cleer's sake I refrained, Lucy. For Cleer's sake I always refrain. You're quite right about that. I know, of course, for Cleer's sake I must keep it locked up in my own heart forever."

The silver-haired lady bent over him again, both caressingly and proudly. "Michael, dear Michael," she said, with a soft thrill in her voice, "I love you and honor you for it. I can FEEL what it costs you. My darling, I know how hard you have to fight against it. I could see you fighting against it to-day; and I was proud of the way you struggled with it, single-handed, till you gained the victory."

Trevennack drew himself up still more haughtily than before. "And who should struggle against the devil," he said, "single-handed as you say, and gain the victory at last, if not I, myself, Lucy?"

He said it like some great one. His wife soothed his hand again and repressed a sigh. She was a great-hearted lady, that brave wife and mother, who bore her own trouble without a word spoken to anyone; but she must sigh, at least, sometimes; it was such a relief to her pent-up feelings. "Who indeed?" she said, acquiescent. "Who indeed, if not you? And I love you best when you conquer so, Michael."

Trevennack looked down upon her with a strange tender look on his face, in which gentleness and condescension were curiously mingled. "Yes," he answered, musing; "for dear Cleer's sake I will always keep my peace about it. I'll say not a word. I'll never tell anybody. And yet it's hard to keep it in; very hard, indeed. I have to bind myself round, as it were, with bonds of iron. The secret will almost out of itself at times. As this morning, for example, when that young fellow wanted to know why St. Michael always clung to such airy pinnacles. How jauntily he talked about it, as if the reason for the selection were a matter of no moment! How little he seemed to think of the Prince of the Archangels!"

"But for Cleer's sake, darling, you kept it in," Mrs. Trevennack said, coaxingly; "and for Cleer's sake you'll keep it in still - I know you will; now won't you?"

Trevennack looked the picture of embodied self-restraint. His back was rigid. "For Cleer's sake I'll keep it in," he said, firmly. "I know how important it is for her. Never in this world have I breathed a word of it to any living soul but you; and never in this world I will. The rest wouldn't understand. They'd say it was madness."

"They would," his wife assented very gravely and earnestly. "And that would be so bad for Cleer's future prospects. People would think you were out of your mind; and you know how chary young men are nowadays of marrying a girl when they believe or even suspect there's insanity in the family. You can talk of it as much and as often as you like to ME, dear Michael. I think that does you good. It acts as a safety-valve. It keeps you from bottling your secret up in your own heart too long, and brooding over it, and worrying yourself. I like you to talk to ME of it whenever you feel inclined. But for heaven's sake, darling, to nobody else. Not a hint of it for worlds. The consequences might be terrible."

Trevennack rose and stood at his full height, with his heels on the edge of the low cottage fender. "You can trust me, Lucy," he said, in a very soft tone, with grave and conscious dignity. "You can trust me to hold my tongue. I know how much depends upon it."

The beautiful lady with the silvery hair sat and gazed on him admiringly. She knew she could trust him; she knew he would keep it in. But she knew at the same time how desperate a struggle the effort cost him; and visionary though he was, she loved and admired him for it.

There was an eloquent silence. Then, after a while, Trevennack spoke again, more tenderly and regretfully. "That man did it!" he said, with slow emphasis. "I saw by his face at once he did it. He killed our poor boy. I could read it in his look. I'm sure it was he. And besides, I have news of it, certain news - from elsewhere," and he looked up significantly.

"Michael!" Mrs. Trevennack said, drawing close to him with an appealing gesture, and gazing hard into his eyes; "it's a long time since. He was a boy at the time. He did it carelessly, no doubt; but not guiltily, culpably. For Cleer's sake, there, too - oh, forgive him, forgive him!" She clasped her hands tight; she looked up at him tearfully.

"It was the devil's work," her husband answered, with a faint frown on his high forehead, "and my task in life, Lucy, is to fight down the devil."

"Fight him down in your own heart, then, dear," Mrs. Trevennack said, gently. "Remember, we all may fall. Lucifer did - and he was once an archangel. Fight him down in your own heart when he suggests hateful thoughts to you. For I know what you felt when it came over you instinctively that that young man had done it. You wanted to fly straight at his throat, dear Michael - you wanted to fly at his throat, and fling him over the precipice."

"I did," Trevennack answered, making no pretense of denial. "But for Cleer's sake I refrained. And for Cleer's sake, if you wish it, I'll try to forgive him."

Mrs. Trevennack pressed his hand. Tears stood in her dim eyes. She, too, had a terrible battle to fight all the days of her life, and she fought it valiantly. "Michael," she said, with an effort, "try to avoid that young man. Try to avoid him, I implore you. Don't go near him in the future. If you see him too often, I'm afraid what the result for you both may be. You control yourself wonderfully, dear; you control yourself, I know; and I'm grateful to you for it. But if you see too much of him, I dread an outbreak. It may get the better of you. And then - think of Cleer! Avoid him! Avoid him!"

For only that silver-headed woman of all people on earth knew the terrible truth, that Michael Trevennack's was a hopeless case of suppressed insanity. Well suppressed, indeed, and kept firmly in check for his daughter's sake, and by his brave wife's aid; but insanity, none the less, of the profoundest monomaniacal pattern, for all that. All day long, and every day, in his dealings with the outer world, he kept down his monomania. An able and trusted government servant, he never allowed it for one moment to interfere with his public duties. To his wife alone he let out what he thought the inmost and deepest secret of his real existence - that he was the Archangel Michael. To no one else did he ever allow a glimpse of the truth, as he thought it, to appear. He knew the world would call it madness; and he didn't wish the stigma of inherited insanity to cling to his Cleer.

Not even Cleer herself for a moment suspected it.

Trevennack was wise enough and cunning enough, as madmen often are, to keep his own counsel, for good and sufficient reason.

Grant Allen

CHAPTER VI

PURE ACCIDENT

During the next week or so, as chance would have it, Cleer Trevennack fell in more than once on her walks with Eustace Le Neve and Walter Tyrrel. They had picked up acquaintance in an irregular way, to be sure; but Cleer hadn't happened to be close by when her father uttered those strange words to his wife, "It was he who did it; it was he who killed our boy"; nor did she notice particularly the marked abruptness of Tyrrel's departure on that unfortunate occasion. So she had no such objection to meeting the two young men as Trevennack himself not unnaturally displayed; she regarded his evident avoidance of Walter Tyrrel as merely one of "Papa's fancies." To Cleer, Papa's fancies were mysterious but very familiar entities; and Tyrrel and Le Neve were simply two interesting and intelligent young men - the squire of the village and a friend on a visit to him. Indeed, to be quite confidential, it was the visitor who occupied the larger share of Cleer's attention. He was so good-looking and so nice. His open face and pink and white complexion had attracted her fancy from the very first; and the more she saw of him the more she liked him.

They met often - quite by accident, of course - on the moor and elsewhere. Tyrrel, for his part, shrank somewhat timidly from the sister of the boy, for his share in whose death he so bitterly reproached himself; yet he couldn't quite drag himself off whenever he found himself in Cleer's presence. She bound him as by a spell. He was profoundly attracted to her. There was something about the pretty Cornish girl so frank, so confiding, in one word, so magnetic, that when once he came near her he couldn't tear himself away as he felt he ought to. Yet he could see very well, none the less, it was for Eustace Le Neve that she watched most eagerly, with the natural interest of a budding girl in the man who takes her pure maiden fancy. Tyrrel allowed with a sigh that this was well indeed; for how could he ever dream, now he knew who she was, of marrying young Michael Trevennack's sister?

One afternoon the two friends were returning from a long ramble across the open moor, when, near a little knoll of bare and weathered rock that rose from a circling belt of Cornish heath, they saw Cleer by herself, propped against the huge boulders, with her eyes fixed intently on a paper-covered novel. She looked up and smiled as they approached; and the young men, turning aside from their ill-marked path, came over and stood by her. They talked for awhile about the ordinary nothings of society small-talk, till by degrees Cleer chanced accidentally to bring the conversation round to something that had happened to her mother and herself a year or two since in Malta. Le Neve snatched at the word; for he was eager to learn all he could about the Trevennacks' movements, so deeply had Cleer already impressed her image on his susceptible nature.

"And when do you go back there?" he asked, somewhat anxiously. "I suppose your father's leave is for a week or two only."

"Oh, dear, no; we don't go back at all, thank heaven," Cleer answered, with a sunny smile. "I can't bear exile, Mr. Le Neve, and I never cared one bit for living in Malta. But this year, fortunately, papa's going to be transferred for a permanence to England; he's to have charge of a department that has something or other to do with provisioning the Channel Squadron; I don't quite understand what; but anyhow, he'll have to be running about between Portsmouth and Plymouth, and I don't know where else; and mamma and I will have to take a house for ourselves in London."

Grant Allen

Le Neve's face showed his pleasure. "That's well," he answered, briskly. "Then you won't be quite lost! I mean, there'll be some chance at least when you go away from here of one's seeing you sometimes."

A bright red spot rose deep on Cleer's cheek through the dark olive-brown skin. "How kind of you to say so," she answered, looking down. "I'm sure mamma'll be very pleased, indeed, if you'll take the trouble to call." Then, to hide her confusion, she went on hastily, "And are YOU going to be in England, too? I thought I understood the other day from your friend you had something to do with a railway in South America."

"Oh, that's all over now," Le Neve answered, with a wave, well pleased she should ask him about his whereabouts so cordially. "I was only employed in the construction of the line, you know; I've nothing at all to do with its maintenance and working, and now the track's laid, my work there's finished. But as to stopping in England, - ah - that's quite another thing. An engineer's, you know, is a roving life. He's here to-day and there to-morrow. I must go, I suppose, wherever work may take me. And there isn't much stirring in the markets just now in the way of engineering."

"I hope you'll get something at home," Cleer said, simply, with a blush, and then blamed herself for saying it. She blushed again at the thought. She looked prettiest when she blushed. Walter Tyrrel, a little behind, stood and admired her all the while. But Eustace was flattered she should think of wanting him to remain in England.

"Thank you," he said, somewhat timidly, for her bashfulness made him a trifle bashful in return. "I should like to very much - for more reasons than one;" and he looked at her meaningly. "I'm getting tired, in some ways, of life abroad. I'd much prefer to come back now and settle down in England."

Cleer rose as he spoke. His frank admiration made her feel self-conscious. She thought this conversation had gone quite far enough for them both for the present. After all, she knew so little of him, though he was really very nice, and he looked at her so kindly! But perhaps it would be better to go and hunt up papa. "I think I ought to be moving now," she said, with a delicious little flush on her smooth, dark cheek. "My father'll be waiting for me." And she set her face across the moor in the opposite direction from the gate of Penmorgan.

"We may come with you, mayn't we?" Eustace asked, with just an undertone of wistfulness.

But Tyrrel darted a warning glance at him. He, at least, couldn't go to confront once more that poor dead boy's father.

"I must hurry home," he said, feebly, consulting his watch with an abstracted air. "It's getting so late. But don't let me prevent YOU from accompanying Miss Trevennack."

Cleer shrank away, a little alarmed. She wasn't quite sure whether it would be perfectly right for her to walk about alone on the moorland with only ONE young man, though she wouldn't have minded the two, for there is safety in numbers. "Oh, no," she said, half frightened, in that composite tone which is at once an entreaty and a positive command. "Don't mind me, Mr. Le Neve. I'm quite accustomed to strolling by myself round the cliff. I wouldn't make you miss your dinner for worlds. And besides, papa's not far off. He went away from me, rambling."

The two young men, accepting their dismissal in the sense in which it was intended, saluted her deferentially, and turned away on their own road. But Cleer took the path to Michael's Crag, by the gully.

From the foot of the crag you can't see the summit. Its own shoulders and the loose rocks of the foreground hide it. But Cleer was pretty certain her father must be there; for he was mostly to be found, when tide permitted it, perched up on the highest pinnacle of his namesake skerry, looking out upon the

Grant Allen

waters with a pre-occupied glance from that airy citadel. The waves in the narrow channel that separate the crag from the opposite mainland were running high and boisterous, but Cleer had a sure foot, and could leap, light as a gazelle, from rock to rock. Not for nothing was she Michael Trevennack's daughter, well trained from her babyhood to high and airy climbs. She chose an easy spot where it was possible to spring across by a series of boulders, arranged accidentally like stepping-stones; and in a minute she was standing on the main crag itself, a huge beetling mass of detached serpentine pushed boldly out as the advance-guard of the land into the assailing waves, and tapering at its top into a pyramidal steeple.

The face of the crag was wet with spray in places; but Cleer didn't mind spray; she was accustomed to the sea in all its moods and tempers. She clambered up the steep side - a sheer wall of bare rock, lightly clad here and there with sparse drapery of green sapphire, or clumps of purple sea-aster, rooted firm in the crannies. Its front was yellow with great patches of lichen, and on the peaks, overhead, the gulls perched, chattering, or launched themselves in long curves upon the evening air. Cleer paused half way up to draw breath and admire the familiar scene. Often as she had gone there before, she could never help gazing with enchanted eyes on those brilliantly colored pinnacles, on that deep green sea, on those angry white breakers that dashed in ceaseless assault against the solid black wall of rock all round her. Then she started once more on her climb up the uncertain path, a mere foothold in the crannies, clinging close with her tiny hands as she went to every jutting corner or weather-worn rock, and every woody stem of weather-beaten sea plants.

At last, panting and hot, she reached the sharp top, expecting to find Trevennack at his accustomed post on the very tallest pinnacle of the craggy little islet. But, to her immense surprise, her father wasn't there. His absence disquieted her. Cleer stood up on the fissured mass of orange-lichened rock that crowned the very summit, dispossessing the gulls who flapped round her as she mounted it; then, shading her eyes with her hand, she looked down in every direction to see if she could descry that missing figure in some nook of the crag. He was nowhere visible. "Father!" she cried aloud, at the top of her voice; "father! father! father!" But the only answer to her cry was the sound of the sea on the base, and the loud noise of the gulls, as they screamed and fluttered in angry surprise over their accustomed breeding-grounds.

Alarmed and irresolute, Cleer sat down on the rock, and facing landwards for awhile, waved her handkerchief to and fro to attract, if possible, her father's attention. Then she scanned the opposite cliffs, beyond the gap or chasm that separated her from the mainland; but she could nowhere see him. He must have forgotten her and gone home to dinner alone, she fancied now, for it was nearly seven o'clock. Nothing remained but to climb down again and follow him. It was getting full late to be out by herself on the island. And tide was coming in, and the surf was getting strong - Atlantic swell from the gale at sea yesterday.

Painfully and toilsomely she clambered down the steep path, making her foothold good, step by step, in the slippery crannies, rendered still more dangerous in places by the sticky spray and the brine that dashed over them from the seething channel. It was harder coming down, a good deal, than going up, and she was accustomed to her father's hand to guide her - to fit her light foot on the little ledges by the way, or to lift her down over the steepest bits with unfailing tenderness. So she found it rather difficult to descend by herself - both difficult and tedious. At last, however, after one or two nasty slips, and a false step or so on the way that ended in her grazing the tender skin on those white little fingers, Cleer reached the base of the crag, and stood face to face with the final problem of crossing the chasm that divided the islet from the opposite mainland.

Then for the first time the truth was borne in upon her with a sudden rush that she couldn't get back - she was imprisoned on the island. She had crossed over at almost the last moment

Grant Allen

possible. The sea now quite covered two or three of her stepping-stones; fierce surf broke over the rest with each advancing billow, and rendered the task of jumping from one to the other impracticable even for a strong and sure-footed man, far more for a slight girl of Cleer's height and figure.

In a moment the little prisoner took in the full horror of the situation. It was now about half tide, and seven o'clock in the evening. High water would therefore fall between ten and eleven; and it must be nearly two in the morning, she calculated hastily, before the sea had gone down enough to let her cross over in safety. Even then, in the dark, she dared hardly face those treacherous stepping-stones. She must stop there till day broke, if she meant to get ashore again without unnecessary hazard.

Cleer was a Trevennack, and therefore brave; but the notion of stopping alone on that desolate island, thronged with gulls and cormorants, in the open air, through all those long dark hours till morning dawned, fairly frightened and appalled her. For a minute or two she crouched and cowered in silence. Then, overcome by terror, she climbed up once more to the first platform of rock, above the reach of the spray, and shouted with all her might, "Father! father! father!"

But 'tis a lonely coast, that wild stretch by the Lizard. Not a soul was within earshot. Cleer sat there still, or stood on top of the crag, for many minutes together, shouting and waving her handkerchief for dear life itself; but not a soul heard her. She might have died there unnoticed; not a creature came near to help or deliver her. The gulls and the cormorants alone stared at her and wondered.

Meanwhile, tide kept flowing with incredible rapidity. The gale in the Atlantic had raised an unwonted swell; and though there was now little wind, the breakers kept thundering in upon the firm, sandy beach with a deafening roar that drowned Cleer's poor voice completely. To add to her misfortunes, fog began to drift slowly with the breeze from seaward. It was getting dark too, and the rocks were damp. Overhead the gulls screamed loud as they flapped and circled above her.

In an agony of despair, Cleer sat down all unnerved on the topmost crag. She began to cry to herself. It was all up now. She knew she must stop there alone till morning.

Grant Allen

CHAPTER VII

PERIL BY LAND

The Trevennacks dined in their lodgings at Gunwalloe at half-past seven. But in the rough open-air life of summer visitors on the Cornish coast, meals as a rule are very movable feasts; and Michael Trevennack wasn't particularly alarmed when he reached home that evening to find Cleer hadn't returned before him. They had missed one another, somehow, among the tangled paths that led down the gully; an easy enough thing to do between those big boulders and bramble-bushes; and it was a quarter to eight before Trevennack began to feel alarmed at Cleer's prolonged absence. By that time, however, he grew thoroughly frightened; and, reproaching himself bitterly for having let his daughter stray out of his sight in the first place, he hurried back, with his wife, at the top of his speed along the cliff path to the Penmorgan headland.

It's half an hour's walk from Gunwalloe to Michael's Crag; and by the time Trevennack reached the mouth of the gully the sands were almost covered; so for the first time in fifteen years he was forced to take the path right under the cliff to the now comparatively distant island, round whose base a whole waste of angry sea surged sullenly. On the way they met a few workmen who, in answer to their inquiries, could give them no news, but who turned back to aid in the search for the missing young lady. When they got opposite Michael's Crag, a wide belt of black water, all encumbered with broken masses of sharp rock, some above and some below the surface, now separated them by fifty yards or more from the island. It was growing dark fast, for these were the closing days of August twilight; and dense fog had drifted in, half obliterating everything. They could barely descry the dim outline of the pyramidal rock in its lower half; its upper part was wholly shrouded in thick mist and drizzle.

With a wild cry of despair, Trevennack raised his voice, and shouted aloud, "Cleer, Cleer! where are you?"

That clarion voice, as of his namesake angel, though raised against the wind, could be heard above even the thud of the fierce breakers that pounded the sand. On the highest peak above, where she sat, cold and shivering, Cleer heard it, and jumped up. "Here! here! father!" she cried out, with a terrible effort, descending at the same time down the sheer face of the cliff as far as the dashing spray and fierce wild waves would allow her.

No other ear caught the sound of that answering cry; but Trevennack's keen senses, preternaturally awakened by the gravity of the crisis, detected the faint ring of her girlish voice through the thunder of the surf. "She's there!" he cried, frantically, waving his hands above his head. "She's there! She's there! We must get across and save her."

For a second Mrs. Trevennack doubted whether he was really right, or whether this was only one of poor Michael's hallucinations. But the next moment, with another cry, Cleer waved her handkerchief in return, and let it fall from her hand. It came, carried on the light breeze, and dropped in the water before their very eyes, half way across the channel.

Frenzied at the sight, Trevennack tore off his coat, and would have plunged into the sea, then and there, to rescue her. But the workmen held him back. "No, no, sir; you mustn't," they said. "No harm can't come to the young lady if she stops there. She've only got to sit on them rocks there till morning, and the tide'll leave her high and dry right enough, as it always do. But nobody couldn't live in such a sea as that - not Tim o' Truro. The waves 'u'd dash him up afore he knowed where he was, and smash him all to pieces on the side o' the island."

Trevennack tried to break from them, but the men held him hard. Their resistance angered him. He chafed under their restraint. How dare these rough fellows lay hands like that on the Prince of the Archangels and a superior officer in Her Majesty's Civil Service? But with the self-restraint that was habitual to him, he managed to refrain, even so, from disclosing his identity. He only struggled ineffectually, instead of blasting them with his hot breath, or clutching his strong arms round their bare throats and choking them. As he stood there and hesitated, half undecided how to act, of a sudden a sharp cry arose from behind. Trevennack turned and looked. Through the dark and the fog he could just dimly descry two men hurrying up, with ropes and life buoys. As they neared him, he started in unspeakable horror. For one of them, indeed, was only Eustace Le Neve; but the other - the other was that devil Walter Tyrrel, who, he felt sure in his own heart, had killed their dear Michael. And it was his task in life to fight and conquer devils.

For a minute he longed to leap upon him and trample him under foot, as long ago he had trampled his old enemy, Satan. What was the fellow doing here now? What business had he with Cleer? Was he always to be in at the death of a Trevennack?

But true to her trust, the silver-haired lady clutched his arm with tender watchfulness. "For Cleer's sake, dear Michael!" she whispered low in his ear; "for Cleer's sake - say nothing; don't speak to him, don't notice him!"

The distracted father drew back a step, out of reach of the spray. "But Lucy," he cried low to her, "only think! only remember! If I cared to go on the cliff and just spread my wings, I could fly across and save her - so instantly, so easily!"

His wife held his hand hard. That touch always soothed him. "If you did, Michael," she said gently, with her feminine tact, "they'd all declare you were mad, and had no wings to fly with. And Cleer's in no immediate danger just now, I feel sure. Don't try, there's a dear man. That's right! Oh, thank you."

Reassured by her calm confidence, Trevennack fell back yet another step on the sands, and watched the men aloof. Walter Tyrrel turned to him. His heart was in his mouth. He spoke in short, sharp sentences. "The coastguard's wife told us," he said. "We've come down to get her off. I've sent word direct to the Lizard lifeboat. But I'm afraid it won't come. They daren't venture out. Sea runs too high, and these rocks are too dangerous."

As he spoke, he tore off his coat, tied a rope round his waist, flung his boots on the sand, and girded himself rapidly with an inflated life-buoy. Then, before the men could seize him or prevent the rash attempt, he had dashed into the great waves that curled and thundered on the beach, and was struggling hard with the sea in a life and death contest. Eustace Le Neve held the rope, and tried to aid him in his endeavors. He had meant to plunge in himself, but Walter Tyrrel was beforehand with him. He was no match in a race against time for the fiery and impetuous Cornish temperament. It wasn't long, however, before the breakers proved themselves more than equal foes for Walter Tyrrel. In another minute he was pounded and pummeled on the unseen rocks under water by the great curling billows. They seized him resistlessly on their crests, tumbled him over like a child, and dashed him, bruised and bleeding, one limp bundle of flesh, against the jagged and pointed summits of the submerged boulders.

With all his might, Eustace Le Neve held on to the rope; then, in coat and boots as he stood, he plunged into the waves and lifted Walter Tyrrel in his strong arms landward. He was a bigger built and more powerful man than his host, and his huge limbs battled harder with the gigantic waves. But even so, in that swirling flood, it was touch and go with him. The breakers lifted him off his feet, tossed him to and fro in their trough, flung him down again forcibly against the sharp-edged rocks, and tried to float off his half unconscious burden. But Le Neve persevered in spite of them, scrambling and tottering as he went, over wet and slippery reefs, with Tyrrel still clasped in his arms, and pressed tight to his breast, till he landed him safe at last on the firm sand beside him.

The squire was far too beaten and bruised by the rocks to make a second attempt against those resistless breakers. Indeed, Le Neve brought him ashore more dead than alive, bleeding from a dozen wounds on the face and hands, and with the breath almost failing in his battered body. They laid him down on the beach, while the fishermen crowded round him, admiring his pluck, though they deprecated his foolhardiness, for they "knowed the squire couldn't never live ag'in it." But Le Neve, still full of the reckless courage of youth, and health, and strength, and manhood, keenly alive now to the peril of Cleer's lonely situation, never heeded their forebodings. He dashed in once more, just as he stood, clothes and all, in the wild and desperate attempt to stem that fierce flood and swim across to the island.

In such a sea as then raged, indeed, and among such broken rocks, swimming, in the strict sense, was utterly impossible. By some mere miracle of dashing about, however - here, battered against the sharp rocks; there, flung over them by the breakers; and yonder, again, sucked down, like a straw in an eddy, by the fierce strength of the undertow - Eustace found himself at last, half unconscious and half choked, carried round by the swirling scour that set through the channel to the south front of the island. Next instant he felt he was cast against the dead wall of rock like an india rubber ball. He rebounded into the trough. The sea caught him a second time, and flung him once more, helpless, against the dripping precipice. With what life was left in him, he clutched with both hands the bare serpentine edge. Good luck befriended him. The great wave had lifted him up on its towering crest to the level of vegetation, beyond the debatable zone. He clung to the hard root of woody sea-aster in the clefts. The waves dashed back in tumultuous little cataracts, and left him there hanging.

Like a mountain goat, Eustace clambered up the side, on hands, knees, feet, elbows, glad to escape with his life from that irresistible turmoil. The treacherous herbs on the slope of the crag were kind to him. He scrambled ahead, like some mad, wild thing. He went onward, upward, cutting his hands at each stage, tearing the skin from his fingers. It was impossible; but he did it. Next minute he found himself high and dry on the island.

His clothes were clinging wet, of course, and his limbs bruised and battered. But he was safe on the firm plateau of the rock at last; and he had rescued Cleer Trevennack!

In the first joy and excitement of the moment he forgot altogether the cramping conventionalities of our every-day life; and, repeating the cry he had heard Michael Trevennack raise from the beach below, he shouted aloud, at the top of his voice, "Cleer! Cleer! Where are you?"

"Here!" came an answering voice from the depths of the gloom overhead. And following the direction whence the sound seemed to come, Eustace Le Neve clambered up to her.

As he seized her hand and wrung it, Cleer crying the while with delight and relief, it struck him all at once, for the very first time, he had done no good by coming, save to give her companionship. It would be hopeless to try carrying her through those intricate rock-channels and that implacable surf, whence he himself had emerged, alone and unburdened, only by a miracle. They two must stop alone there on the rock till morning.

As for Cleer, too innocent and too much of a mere woman in her deadly peril to think of anything but the delightful sense of confidence in a strong man at her side to guard and protect her, she sat and held his hand still, in a perfect transport of gratitude. "Oh, how good of you to come!" she cried again and again, bending over it in her relief, and half tempted to kiss it. "How good of you to come across like that to save me."

CHAPTER VIII

SAFE AT LAST

The night was long. The night was dark. Slowly the fog closed them in. It grew rainier and more dismal. But on the summit of the crag Eustace Le Neve stood aloft, and waved his arms, and shouted. He lit a match and shaded it. The dull glare of it through the mist just faintly reached the eyes of the anxious watchers on the beach below. From a dozen lips there rose an answering shout. The pair on the crag half heard its last echoes. Eustace put his hands to his mouth and cried aloud once more, in stentorian tones, "All right. Cleer's here. We can hold out till morning."

Trevennack alone heard the words. But he repeated them so instantly that his wife felt sure it was true hearing, not insane hallucination. The sea was gaining on them now. It had risen almost up to the face of the cliffs. Reluctantly they turned along the path by the gully, and mounting the precipice waited and watched till morning on the tor that overlooks Michael's Crag from the Penmorgan headland.

Every now and again, through that livelong night, Trevennack whispered in his wife's ear, "If only I chose to spread my wings, and launch myself, I could fly across and carry her." And each time that brave woman, holding his hand in her own and smoothing it gently, answered in her soft voice, "But then the secret would be out, and Cleer's life would be spoiled, and they'd call you a madman. Wait till morning, dear Michael;

do, do, wait till morning."

And Trevennack, struggling hard with the mad impulse in his heart, replied with all his soul, "I will; I will; for Cleer's sake and yours, I'll try to keep it down. I'll not be mad. I'll be strong and restrain it."

For he knew he was insane, in his inmost soul, almost as well as he knew his name was Michael the Archangel.

On the island, meanwhile, Eustace Le Neve and Cleer Trevennack sat watching out the weary night, and longing for the dawn to make the way back possible. At least, Cleer did, for as to Eustace, in spite of rain and fog and cold and darkness, he was by no means insensible to the unwonted pleasure of so long a tete-a-tete, in such romantic circumstances, with the beautiful Cornish girl. To be sure the waves roared, and the drizzle dripped, and the seabirds flapped all round them. But many waters will not quench love. Cleer was by his side, holding his hand in hers in the dark for pure company's sake, because she was so frightened; and as the night wore on they talked at last of many things. They were prisoners there for five mortal hours or so, alone, together; and they might as well make the best of it by being sociable with one another.

There could be no denying, however, that it was cold and damp and dark and uncomfortable. The rain came beating down upon them, as they sat there side by side on that exposed rock. The spray from the breakers blew in with the night wind; the light breeze struck chill on their wet clothes and faces. After awhile Eustace began a slow tour of inspection over the crag, seeking some cave or rock shelter, some projecting ledge of stone on the leeward side that might screen their backs at least from the driving showers. Cleer couldn't be left alone; she clung to his hand as he felt his way about the islet, with uncertain steps, through the gloom and fog. Once he steadied himself on a jutting piece of the rock as he supposed, when to his immense surprise - wh'r'r'r - it rose from under his hand, with a shrill cry of alarm, and fluttered wildly seaward. It was some sleeping gull, no doubt, disturbed unexpectedly in its accustomed resting-place. Eustace staggered and almost fell. Cleer supported him with her arm. He accepted her aid gratefully. They stumbled on in the dark once more, lighting now and again for a minute or two one of his six precious matches - he had no more in his case - and exploring as well as they might the whole broken surface of that fissured pinnacle. "I'm so glad you smoke, Mr. Le Neve," Cleer said, simply, as he lit one. "For if you didn't, you know, we'd have been left here all night in utter darkness."

At last, in a nook formed by the weathered joints, Eustace found a rugged niche, somewhat dryer than the rest, and laid Cleer gently down in it, on a natural spring seat of tufted rock-plants. Then he settled down beside her, with what cheerfulness he could muster up, and taking off his wet coat, spread it on top across the cleft, like a tent roof, to shelter them. It was no time, indeed, to stand upon ceremony. Cleer recognized as much, and nestled close to his side, like a sensible girl as she was, so as to keep warm by mere company; while Eustace, still holding her hand, just to assure her of his presence, placed himself in such an attitude, leaning before her and above her, as to protect her as far as possible from the drizzling rainfall through the gap in front of them. There they sat till morning, talking gradually of many things, and growing more and more confidential, in spite of cold and wet, as they learnt more and more, with each passing hour, of each other's standpoint. There are some situations where you get to know people better in a few half-hours together than you could get to know them in months upon months of mere drawing-room acquaintance. And this was one of them. Before morning dawned, Eustace Le Neve and Cleer Trevennack felt just as if they had known one another quite well for years. They were old and trusted friends already. Old friends - and even something more than that. Though no word of love was spoken between them, each knew of what the other was thinking. Eustace felt Cleer loved him; Cleer felt Eustace loved her. And in spite of rain and cold and fog and darkness they were almost happy - before dawn came to interrupt their strange tete-a-tete on the islet.

As soon as day broke Eustace looked out from their eyrie on the fissured peak, and down upon the troubled belt of water below. The sea was now ebbing, and the passage between the rock and the mainland though still full (for it was never dry even at spring-tide low water) was fairly passable by this time over the natural bridge of stepping-stones. He clambered down the side, giving his hand to Cleer from ledge to ledge as he went. The fog had lifted a little, and on the opposite headland they could just dimly descry the weary watchers looking eagerly out for them. Eustace put his hands to his mouth, and gave a loud halloo. The sound of the breakers was less deafening now; his voice carried to the mainland. Trevennack, who had sat under a tarpaulin through the livelong night, watching and waiting with anxious heart for the morning, raised an answering shout, and waved his hat in his hand frantically. St. Michael's Crag had not betrayed its trust. That was the motto of the Trevennacks - "Stand fast, St. Michael's!" - under the crest of the rocky islet, castled and mured, flamboyant. Eustace reached the bottom of the rock, and, wading in the water himself, or jumping into the deepest parts, helped Cleer across the stepping-stones. Meanwhile, the party on the cliff had hurried down by the gully path; and a minute later Cleer was in her mother's arms, while Trevennack held her hand, inarticulate with joy, and bent over her eagerly.

"Oh, mother," Cleer cried, in her simple girlish naivete, "Mr. Le Neve's been so kind to me! I don't know how I should ever have got through the night without him. It was so good of him to come. He's been SUCH a help to me."

The father and mother both looked into her eyes - a single searching glance - and understood perfectly. They grasped Le Neve's hand. Tears rolled down their cheeks. Not a word was spoken, but in a certain silent way all four understood one another.

"Where's Tyrrel?" Eustace asked.

And Mrs. Trevennack answered, "Carried home, severely hurt. He was bruised on the rocks. But we hope not dangerously. The doctor's been to see him, we hear, and finds no bones broken. Still, he's terribly battered about, in those fearful waves, and it must be weeks, they tell us, before he can quite recover."

But Cleer, as was natural, thought more of the man who had struggled through and reached her than of the man who had failed in the attempt, though he suffered all the more for it. This is a world of the successful. In it, as in most other planets I have visited, people make a deal more fuss over the smallest success than over the noblest failure.

It was no moment for delay. Eustace turned on his way at once, and ran up to Penmorgan. And the Trevennacks returned, very wet and cold, in the dim gray dawn to their rooms at Gunwalloe.

As soon as they were alone - Cleer put safely to bed - Trevennack looked at his wife. "Lucy," he said, slowly, in a disappointed tone, "after this, of course, come what may, they must marry."

"They must," his wife answered. "There's no other way left. And fortunately, dear, I could see from the very first, Cleer likes him, and he likes her."

The father paused a moment. It wasn't quite the match he had hoped for a Trevennack of Trevennack. Then he added, very fervently, "Thank God it was HIM - not that other man, Tyrrel! Thank God, the first one fell in the water and was hurt. What should we ever have done - oh, what should we have done, Lucy, if she'd been cut off all night long on that lonely crag face to face with the man who murdered our dear boy Michael?"

Mrs. Trevennack drew a long breath. Then she spoke earnestly once more. "Dear heart," she said, looking deep into his clear brown eyes, "now remember, more than ever, Cleer's future is at stake. For Cleer's sake, more than ever, keep a guard on yourself, Michael; watch word and deed, do nothing foolish."

"You can trust me!" Trevennack answered, drawing himself up to his full height, and looking proudly before him. "Cleer's future is at stake. Cleer has a lover now. Till Cleer is married, I'll give you my sacred promise no living soul shall ever know in any way she's an archangel's daughter."

CHAPTER IX

MEDICAL OPINION

From that day forth, by some unspoken compact, it was "Eustace" and "Cleer," wherever they met, between them. Le Neve began it, by coming round in the afternoon of that self-same day, as soon as he'd slept off the first effects of his fatigue and chill, to inquire of Mrs. Trevennack "how Cleer was getting on" after her night's exposure. And Mrs. Trevennack accepted the frank usurpation in very good part, as indeed was no wonder, for Cleer had wanted to know half an hour before whether "Eustace" had yet been round to ask after her. The form of speech told all. There was no formal engagement, and none of the party knew exactly how or when they began to take it for granted; but from that evening on Michael's Crag it was a tacitly accepted fact between Le Neve and the Trevennacks that Eustace was to marry Cleer as soon as he could get a permanent appointment anywhere.

Engineering, however, is an overstocked profession. In that particular it closely resembles most other callings.

The holidays passed away, and Walter Tyrrel recovered, and the Trevennacks returned to town for the head of the house to take up his new position in the Admiralty service; but Eustace Le Neve heard of no opening anywhere for an energetic young man with South American experience. Those three years he had passed out of England, indeed, had made him lose touch with other members of his craft. People shrugged their

Grant Allen

shoulders when they heard of him, and opined, with a chilly smile, he was the sort of young man who ought to go to the colonies. That's the easiest way of shelving all similar questions. The colonies are popularly regarded in England as the predestined dumping-ground for all the fools and failures of the mother-country. So Eustace settled down in lodgings in London, not far from the Trevennacks, and spent more of his time, it must be confessed, in going round to see Cleer than in perfecting himself in the knowledge of his chosen art. Not that he failed to try every chance that lay open to him - he had far too much energy to sit idle in his chair and let the stream of promotion flow by unattempted; but chances were few and applicants were many, and month after month passed away to his chagrin without the clever young engineer finding an appointment anywhere. Meanwhile, his little nest-egg of South-American savings was rapidly disappearing; and though Tyrrel, who had influence with railway men, exerted himself to the utmost on his friend's behalf - partly for Cleer's sake, and partly for Eustace's own - Le Neve saw his balance growing daily smaller, and began to be seriously alarmed at last, not merely for his future prospects of employment and marriage, but even for his immediate chance of a modest livelihood.

Nor was Mrs. Trevennack, for her part, entirely free from sundry qualms of conscience as to her husband's condition and the rightfulness of concealing it altogether from Cleer's accepted lover. Trevennack himself was so perfectly sane in every ordinary relation of life, so able a business head, so dignified and courtly an English gentleman, that Eustace never even for a moment suspected any undercurrent of madness in that sound practical intelligence. Indeed, no man could talk with more absolute common sense about his daughter's future, or the duties and functions of an Admiralty official, than Michael Trevennack. It was only to his wife in his most confidential moments that he ever admitted the truth as to his archangelic character; to all others whom he met he was simply a distinguished English civil servant of blameless life and very solid judgment. The heads of his department placed the most implicit trust in Trevennack's opinion; there was no man about the place who could decide a knotty point of detail off-hand like Michael Trevennack. What was his poor wife to do, then? Was it her place to warn Eustace that Cleer's father might at any moment unexpectedly develop symptoms of dangerous insanity? Was she bound thus to wreck her own daughter's happiness? Was she bound to speak out the very secret of her heart which she had spent her whole life in inducing Trevennack himself to bottle up with ceaseless care in his distracted bosom?

And yet ... she saw the other point of view as well - alas, all too plainly. She was a martyr to conscience, like Walter Tyrrel himself; was it right of her, then, to tie Eustace for life to a girl who was really a madman's daughter? This hateful question was up before her often in the dead dark night, as she lay awake on her bed, tossing and turning feverishly; it tortured her in addition to her one lifelong trouble. For the silver-haired lady had borne the burden of that unknown sorrow locked up in her own bosom for fifteen years; and it had left on her face such a beauty of holiness as a great trouble often leaves indelibly stamped on women of the same brave, loving temperament.

One day, about three months later, in their drawing-room at Bayswater, Eustace Le Neve happened to let drop a casual remark which cut poor Mrs. Trevennack to the quick, like a knife at her heart. He was talking of some friend of his who had lately got engaged. "It's a terrible thing," he said, seriously. "There's insanity in the family. I wouldn't marry into such a family as that - no, not if I loved a girl to distraction, Mrs. Trevennack. The father's in a mad-house, you know; and the girl's very nice now, but one never can tell when the tendency may break out. And then - just think! what an inheritance to hand on to one's innocent children!"

Trevennack took no open notice of what he said. But Mrs. Trevennack winced, grew suddenly pale, and stammered out some conventional none-committing platitude. His words entered her very soul. They stung and galled her. That night she lay awake and thought more bitterly to herself about the matter than ever. Next morning early, as soon as Trevennack had set off to catch the fast train from Waterloo to Portsmouth direct (he was frequently down there on Admiralty business), she put on her cloak and bonnet, without a word to Cleer, and set out in a hansom all alone to Harley Street.

The house to which she drove was serious-looking and professional - in point of fact, it was Dr. Yate-Westbury's, the well-known specialist on mental diseases. She sent up no card and gave no name. On the contrary, she kept her veil down - and it was a very thick one. But Dr. Yate-Westbury made no comment on this reticence; it was a familiar occurrence with him - people are often ashamed to have it known they consult a mad-doctor.

"I want to ask you about my husband's case," Mrs. Trevennack began, trembling. And the great specialist, all attention, leaned forward and listened to her.

Mrs. Trevennack summoned up courage, and started from the very beginning. She described how her husband, who was a government servant, had been walking below a cliff on the seashore with their only son, some fifteen years earlier, and how a shower of stones from the top had fallen on their heads and killed their poor boy, whose injuries were the more serious. She could mention it all now with comparatively little emotion; great sorrows since had half obliterated that first and greatest one. But she laid stress upon the point that her husband had been struck, too, and was very gravely hurt - so gravely, indeed, that it was weeks before he recovered physically.

"On what part of the head?" Yate-Westbury asked, with quick medical insight.

And Mrs. Trevennack answered, "Here," laying her small gloved hand on the center of the left temple.

The great specialist nodded. "Go on," he said, quietly. "Fourth frontal convolution! And it was a month or two, I have no doubt, before you noticed any serious symptoms supervening?"

"Exactly so," Mrs. Trevennack made answer, very much relieved. "It was all of a month or two. But from that day forth - from the very beginning, I mean - he had a natural horror of going BENEATH a cliff, and he liked to get as high up as he could, so as to be perfectly sure there was nobody at all anywhere above to hurt him." And then she went on to describe in short but graphic phrase how he loved to return to the place of his son's accident, and to stand for hours on lonely sites overlooking the spot, and especially on a crag which was dedicated to St. Michael.

The specialist caught at what was coming with the quickness, she thought, of long experience. "Till he fancied himself the archangel?" he said, promptly and curiously.

Mrs. Trevennack drew a deep breath of satisfaction and relief. "Yes," she answered, flushing hot. "Till he fancied himself the archangel. There - there were extenuating circumstances, you see. His own name's Michael; and his family - well, his family have a special connection with St. Michael's Mount; their crest's a castled crag with 'Stand fast, St. Michael's!' and he knew he had to fight against this mad impulse of his own - which he felt was like a devil within him - for his daughter's sake; and he was always standing alone on these rocky high places, dedicated to St. Michael, till the fancy took full hold upon him; and now, though he knows in a sort of a way he's mad, he believes quite firmly he's St. Michael the Archangel."

Yate-Westbury nodded once more. "Precisely the development I should expect to occur," he said, "after such an accident."

Mrs. Trevennack almost bounded from her seat in her relief. "Then you attribute it to the accident first of all?" she asked, eagerly.

"Not a doubt about it," the specialist answered. "The region you indicate is just the one where similar illusory ideas are apt to arise from external injuries. The bruise gave the cause, and circumstances the form. Besides, the case is normal - quite normal altogether. Does he have frequent outbreaks?"

Mrs. Trevennack explained that he never had any. Except to herself, and that but seldom, he never alluded to the subject in any way.

Yate-Westbury bit his lip. "He must have great self-control," he answered, less confidently. "In a case like that, I'm bound to admit, my prognosis - for the final result - would be most unfavorable. The longer he bottles it up the more terrible is the outburst likely to be when it arrives. You must expect that some day he will break out irrepressibly."

Mrs. Trevennack bowed her head with the solemn placidity of despair. "I'm quite prepared for that," she said, quietly; "though I try hard to delay it, for a specific reason. That wasn't the question I came to consult you about to-day. I feel sure my poor husband's case is perfectly hopeless, as far as any possibility of cure is concerned; what I want to know is about another aspect of the case." She leaned forward appealingly. "Oh, doctor," she cried, clasping her hands, "I have a dear daughter at home - the one thing yet left me. She's engaged to be married to a young man whom she loves - a young man who loves her. Am I bound to tell him she's a madman's child? Is there any chance of its affecting her? Is the taint hereditary?"

She spoke with deep earnestness. She rushed out with it without reserve. Yate-Westbury gazed at her compassionately. He was a kind-hearted man. "No; certainly not," he answered, with emphasis. "Not the very slightest reason in any way to fear it. The sanest man, coming from the very sanest and healthiest stock on earth, would almost certainly be subject to delusions under such circumstances. This is accident, not disease - circumstance, not temperament. The injury to the brain is the result of a special blow. Grief for the loss of his son, and brooding over the event, no doubt contributed to the particular shape the delusion has assumed. But the injury's the main thing. I don't doubt there's a clot of blood formed just here on the brain, obstructing its functions in part, and disturbing its due relations. In every other way, you say, he's a good man of business. The very apparent rationality of the delusion - the way it's been led up to by his habit of standing on cliffs, his name, his associations, his family, everything - is itself a good sign that the partial insanity is due to a local and purely accidental cause. It simulates reason as closely as possible. Dismiss the question altogether from your mind, as far as your daughter's future is concerned. Its no more likely to be inherited than a broken leg or an amputated arm is."

Mrs. Trevennack burst into a flood of joyous tears. "Then all I have to do," she sobbed out, "is to keep him from an outbreak until after my daughter's married."

Dr. Yate-Westbury nodded. "That's all you have to do," he answered, sympathetically. "And I'm sure Mrs. Trevennack -" he paused with a start and checked himself.

"Why, how do you know my name?" the astonished mother cried, drawing back with a little shudder of half superstitious alarm at such surprising prescience.

Dr. Yate-Westbury made a clean breast of it. "Well, to tell the truth," he said, "Mr. Trevennack himself called round here yesterday, in the afternoon, and stated the whole case to me from his own point of view, giving his name in full - as a man would naturally do - but never describing to me the nature of his delusion. He said it was too sacred a thing for him to so much as touch upon; that he knew he wasn't mad, but that the world would think him so; and he wanted to know, from something he'd heard said, whether madness caused by an injury of the sort would or would not be considered by medical men as inheritable. And I told him at once, as I've told you to-day, there was not the faintest danger of it. But I never made such a slip in my life before as blurting out the name. I

Grant Allen

could only have done it to you. Trust me, your secret is safe in my keeping. I have hundreds in my head." He took her hand in his own as he spoke. "Dear madam," he said, gently," I understand; I feel for you."

"Thank you," Mrs. Trevennack answered low, with tears standing in her eyes. "I'm - I'm so glad you've SEEN him. It makes your opinion so much more valuable to me. But you thought his delusion wholly due to the accident, then?"

"Wholly due to the accident, dear lady. Yes, wholly, wholly due to it. You may go home quite relieved. Your doubts and fears are groundless. Miss Trevennack may marry with a clear conscience."

CHAPTER X

A BOLD ATTEMPT

During the next ten or eleven months poor Mrs. Trevennack had but one abiding terror - that a sudden access of irrepressible insanity might attack her husband before Cleer and Eustace could manage to get married. Trevennack, however, with unvarying tenderness, did his best in every way to calm her fears. Though no word on the subject passed between them directly, he let her feel with singular tact that he meant to keep himself under proper control. Whenever a dangerous topic cropped up in conversation, he would look across at her affectionately, with a reassuring smile. "For Cleer's sake," he murmured often, if she was close by his side; "for Cleer's sake, dearest!" and his wife, mutely grateful, knew at once what he meant, and smiled approval sadly.

Her heart was very full; her part was a hard one to play with fitting cheerfulness; but in his very madness itself she couldn't help loving, admiring, and respecting that strong, grave husband who fought so hard against his own profound convictions.

Ten months passed away, however, and Eustace Le Neve didn't seem to get much nearer any permanent appointment than ever. He began to tire at last of applying unsuccessfully for every passing vacancy. Now and then he got odd jobs, to be sure; but odd jobs won't do for a man to marry upon; and serious work seemed always to elude him. Walter Tyrrel did

Grant Allen

his best, no doubt, to hunt up all the directors of all the companies he knew; but no posts fell vacant on any line they were connected with. It grieved Walter to the heart, for he had always had the sincerest friendship for Eustace Le Neve; and now that Eustace was going to marry Cleer Trevennack, Walter felt himself doubly bound in honor to assist him. It was HE who had ruined the Trevennacks' hopes in life by his unintentional injury to their only son; the least he could do in return, he thought, and felt, was to make things as easy as possible for their daughter and her intended husband.

By July, however, things were looking so black for the engineer's prospects that Tyrrel made up his mind to run up to town and talk things over seriously with Eustace Le Neve himself in person. He hated going up there, for he hardly knew how he could see much of Eustace without running some risk of knocking up accidentally against Michael Trevennack; and there was nothing on earth that sensitive young squire dreaded so much as an unexpected meeting with the man he had so deeply, though no doubt so unintentionally and unwittingly, injured. But he went, all the same. He felt it was his duty. And duty to Walter Tyrrel spoke in an imperative mood which he dared not disobey, however much he might be minded to turn a deaf ear to it.

Le Neve had little to suggest of any practical value. It wasn't his fault, Tyrrel knew; engineering was slack, and many good men were looking out for appointments. In these crowded days, it's a foolish mistake to suppose that energy, industry, ability, and integrity are necessarily successful. To insure success you must have influence, opportunity, and good luck as well, to back them. Without these, not even the invaluable quality of unscrupulousness itself is secure from failure.

If only Walter Tyrrel could have got his friend to accept such terms, indeed, he would gladly, for Cleer's sake, have asked Le Neve to marry on an allowance of half the Penmorgan rent-roll. But in this commercial age, such quixotic arrangements are simply impossible. So Tyrrel set to work with fiery zeal to find out what openings were just then to be had; and first of all for that purpose he went to call on a parliamentary friend of his, Sir Edward Jones, the fat and good-natured chairman of the Great North Midland Railway. Tyrrel was a shareholder whose vote was worth considering, and he supported the Board with unwavering loyalty.

Sir Edward was therefore all attention, and listened with sympathy to Tyrrel's glowing account of his friend's engineering energy and talent. When he'd finished his eulogy, however, the practical railway magnate crossed his fat hands and put in, with very common-sense dryness, "If he's so clever as all that, why doesn't he have a shot at this Wharfedale Viaduct?"

Walter Tyrrel drew back a little surprised. The Wharfedale Viaduct was a question just then in everybody's mouth. But what a question! Why, it was one of the great engineering works of the age; and it was informally understood that the company were prepared to receive plans and designs from any competent person. There came the rub, though. Would Eustace have a chance in such a competition as that? Much as he believed in his old school-fellow, Tyrrel hesitated and reflected. "My friend's young, of course," he said, after a pause. "He's had very little experience - comparatively, I mean - to the greatness of the undertaking."

Sir Edward pursed his fat lips. It's a trick with your railway kings. "Well, young men are often more inventive than old ones," he answered, slowly. "Youth has ideas; middle age has experience. In a matter like this, my own belief is, the ideas count for most. Yes, if I were you, Tyrrel, I'd ask your friend to consider it."

"You would?" Walter cried, brightening up.

"Aye, that I would," the great railway-man answered, still more confidently than before, rubbing his fat hands reflectively. "It's a capital opening. Erasmus Walker'll be in for it, of course; and

Grant Allen

Erasmus Walker'll get it. But don't you tell your fellow that. It'll only discourage him. You just send him down to Yorkshire to reconnoiter the ground; and if he's good for anything, when he's seen the spot he'll make a plan of his own, a great deal better than Walker's. Not that that'll matter, don't you know, as far as this viaduct goes. The company'll take Walker's, no matter how good any other fellow's may be, and how bad Walker's - because Walker has a great name, and because they think they can't go far wrong if they follow Walker. But still, if your friend's design is a good one, it'll attract attention - which is always something; and after they've accepted Walker's, and flaws begin to be found in it - as experts can always find flaws in anything, no matter how well planned - your friend can come forward and make a fuss in the papers (or what's better still, YOU can come forward and make it for him) to say these flaws were strikingly absent from HIS very superior and scientific conception. There'll be flaws in your friend's as well, of course, but they won't be the same ones, and nobody'll have the same interest in finding them out and exposing them. And that'll get your man talked about in the papers and the profession. It's better, anyhow, than wasting his time doing nothing in London here."

"He shall do it!" Walter cried, all on fire. "I'll take care he shall do it. And Sir Edward, I tell you, I'd give five thousand pounds down if only he could get the job away from Walker."

"Got a grudge against Walker, then?" Sir Edward cried quickly, puckering up his small eyes.

"Oh, no," Tyrrel answered, smiling; that was not much in his line. "But I've got strong reasons of my own, on the other hand, for wishing to do a good turn to Le Neve in this business."

And he went home, reflecting in his own soul on the way that many thousands would be as dross in the pan to him if only he could make Cleer Trevennack happy.

But that very same evening Trevennack came home from the Admiralty in a most excited condition.

"Lucy!" he cried to his wife, as soon as he was alone in the room with her, "who do you think I saw to-day - there, alive in the flesh, standing smiling on the steps of Sir Edward Jones' house? - that brute Walter Tyrrel, who killed our poor boy for us!" "Hush! hush, Michael!" his wife cried in answer. "It's so long ago now, and he was such a boy at the time; and he repents it bitterly - I'm sure he repents it. You promised you'd try to forgive him. For Cleer's sake, dear heart, you must keep your promise."

Trevennack knit his brows. "What does he mean, then, by dogging my steps?" he cried. "What does he mean by coming after me up to London like this? What does he mean by tempting me? I can't stand the sight of him. I won't be challenged, Lucy; I don't know whether it's the devil or not, but when I saw the fellow to-day I had hard work to keep my hands off him. I wanted to spring at his throat. I would have liked to throttle him!"

The silver-haired lady drew still closer to the excited creature, and held his hands with a gentle pressure. "Michael," she said, earnestly, "this IS the devil. This is the greatest temptation of all. This is what I dread most for you. Remember, it's Satan himself that suggests such thoughts to you. Fight the devil WITHIN, dearest. Fight him within, like a man. That's the surest place, after all, to conquer him."

Trevennack drew himself up proudly, and held his peace for a time. Then he went on in another tone: "I shall get leave," said he quietly, becoming pure human once more. "I shall get leave of absence. I can't stop in town while this creature's about. I'd HAVE to spring at him if I saw him again. I can't keep my hands off him. I'll fly from temptation. I must go down into the country."

"Not to Cornwall!" Mrs. Trevennack cried, in deep distress;

for she dreaded the effect of those harrowing associations for him.

Trevennack shook his head gravely. "No, not to Cornwall," he answered. "I've another plan this time. I want to go to Dartmoor. It's lonely enough there. Not a soul to distract me. You know, Lucy, when one means to fight the devil, there's nothing for it like the wilderness; and Dartmoor's wilderness enough for me. I shall go to Ivybridge, for the tors and the beacons."

Mrs. Trevennack assented gladly. If he wanted to fight the devil, it was best at any rate he should be out of reach of Walter Tyrrel while he did it. And it was a good thing to get him away, too, from St. Michael's Mount, and St. Michael's Crag, and St. Michael's Chair, and all the other reminders of his archangelic dignity in the Penzance neighborhood. Why, she remembered with a wan smile - the dead ghost of a smile rather - he couldn't even pass the Angel Inn at Helston without explaining to his companions that the parish church was dedicated to St. Michael, and that the swinging sign of the old coaching house once bore a picture of the winged saint himself in mortal conflict with his Satanic enemy. It was something, at any rate, to get Trevennack away from a district so replete with memories of his past greatness, to say nothing of the spot where their poor boy had died. But Mrs. Trevennack didn't know that one thing which led her husband to select Dartmoor this time for his summer holiday was the existence, on the wild hills a little behind Ivybridge, of a clatter-crowned peak, known to all the country-side as St. Michael's Tor, and crowned in earlier days by a medieval chapel. It was on this sacred site of his antique cult that Trevennack wished to fight the internal devil. And he would fight it with a will, on that he was resolved; fight and, as became his angelic reputation, conquer.

CHAPTER XI

BUSINESS IS BUSINESS

It reconciled Cleer to leaving London for awhile when she learnt that Eustace Le Neve was going north to Yorkshire, with Walter Tyrrel, to inspect the site of the proposed Wharfedale viaduct. Not that she ever mentioned his companion's name in her father's presence. Mrs. Trevennack had warned her many times over, with tears in her eyes, but without cause assigned, never to allude to Tyrrel's existence before her father's face; and Cleer, though she never for one moment suspected the need for such reticence, obeyed her mother's injunction with implicit honesty. So they parted two ways, Eustace and Tyrrel for the north, the Trevennacks for Devonshire. Cleer needed a change indeed; she'd spent the best part of a year in London. And for Cleer, that was a wild and delightful holiday. Though Eustace wasn't there, to be sure, he wrote hopefully from the north; he was maturing his ideas; he was evolving a plan; the sense of the magnitude of his stake in this attempt had given him an unwonted outburst of inspiration. As she wandered with her father among those boggy uplands, or stood on the rocky tors that so strangely crest the low flat hill-tops of the great Devonian moor. She felt a marvelous exhilaration stir her blood - the old Cornish freedom making itself felt through all the restrictions of our modern civilization. She was to the manner born, and she loved the Celtic West Country.

But to Michael Trevennack it was life, health, vigor. He hated London. He hated officialdom. He hated the bonds of red tape

Grant Allen

that enveloped him. It's hard to know yourself an archangel -

"One of the seven who nearest to the throne
Stand ready at command, and are as eyes
That run through all the heavens, or down to the earth,"

and yet to have to sit at a desk all day long, with a pen in your hand, in obedience to the orders of the First Lord of the Admiralty! It's hard to know you can

"Bear swift errands over moist and dry,
O'er sea and land,"

as his laureate Milton puts it, and yet be doomed to keep still hour after hour in a stuffy office, or to haggle over details of pork and cheese in a malodorous victualing yard. Trevennack knew his "Paradise Lost" by heart - it was there, indeed, that he had formed his main ideas of the archangelic character; and he repeated the sonorous lines to himself, over and over again, in a ringing, loud voice, as he roamed the free moor or poised light on the craggy pinnacles. This was the world that he loved, these wild rolling uplands, these tall peaks of rock, these great granite boulders; he had loved them always, from the very beginning of things; had he not poised so of old, ages and ages gone by, on that famous crag

"Of alabaster, piled up to the clouds,
Conspicuous far, winding with one ascent
Accessible from earth, one entrance high;
The rest was craggy cliff that overhung
Still as it rose, impossible to climb."

So he had poised in old days; so he poised himself now, with Cleer by
his side, an angel confessed, on those high tors of Dartmoor.

But amid all the undulations of that great stony ocean, one peak there was that delighted Trevennack's soul more than any of the rest - a bold russet crest, bursting suddenly through the heathery waste in abrupt ascent, and scarcely to be scaled, save on one difficult side, like its Miltonic prototype. Even Cleer, who accompanied her father everywhere on his rambles, clad in stout shoes and coarse blue serge gown - . for Dartmoor is by no means a place to be approached by those who, like Agag, "walk delicately" - even Cleer didn't know that this craggy peak, jagged and pointed like some Alpine or dolomitic aiguille, was known to all the neighboring shepherds around as St. Michael's Tor, from its now forgotten chapel. A few wild Moorland sheep grazed now and again on the short herbage at its base; but for the most part father and daughter found themselves alone amid that gorse-clad solitude. There Michael Trevennack would stand erect, with head bare and brows knit, in the full eye of the sun, for hour after hour at a time, fighting the devil within him. And when he came back at night, tired out with his long tramp across the moor and his internal struggle, he would murmur to his wife, "I've conquered him to-day. It was a hard, hard fight! But I conquered! I conquered him!"

Up in the north, meanwhile, Eustace Le Neve worked away with a will at the idea for his viaduct. As he rightly wrote to Cleer, the need itself inspired him. Love is a great engineer, and Eustace learned fast from him. He was full of the fresh originality of youth; and the place took his fancy and impressed itself upon him. Gazing at it each day, there rose up slowly by degrees in his mind, like a dream, the picture of a great work on a new and startling principle - a modification of the cantilever to the necessities of the situation. Bit by bit he worked it out, and reduced his first floating conception to paper; then he explained it to Walter Tyrrel, who listened hard to his explanations, and tried his best to understand the force of the technical arguments. Enthusiasm is catching; and Le Neve was enthusiastic about his imaginary viaduct, till Walter Tyrrel in turn grew almost as enthusiastic as the designer himself over its beauty and utility. So charmed was he with the idea, indeed, that when Le Neve had at last committed it all to paper, he couldn't resist the temptation of asking leave to show it to Sir Edward Jones, whom he had already consulted as to

Eustace's prospects.

Eustace permitted him, somewhat reluctantly, to carry the design to the great railway king, and on the very first day of their return to London, in the beginning of October, Tyrrel took the papers round to Sir Edward's house in Onslow Gardens. The millionaire inspected it at first with cautious reserve. He was a good business man, and he hated enthusiasm - except in money matters. But gradually, as Walter Tyrrel explained to him the various points in favor of the design, Sir Edward thawed. He looked into it carefully. Then he went over the calculations of material and expense with a critical eye. At the end he leant back in his study chair, with one finger on the elevation and one eye on the figures, while he observed with slow emphasis: "This is a very good design. Why, man, its just about twenty times better than Erasmus Walker's."

"Then you think it may succeed?" Tyrrel cried, with keen delight, as anxious for Cleer's sake as if the design were his own. "You think they may take it?"

"Oh dear, no," Sir Edward answered, confidently, with a superior smile. "Not the slightest chance in the world of that. They'd never even dream of it. It's novel, you see, novel, while Walker's is conventional. And they'll take the conventional one. But its a first rate design for all that, I can tell you. I never saw a better one."

"Well, but how do you know what Walker's is like?" Tyrrel asked, somewhat dismayed at the practical man's coolness.

"Oh, he showed it me last night," Sir Edward answered, calmly. "A very decent design, on the familiar lines, but not fit to hold a candle to Le Neve's, of course; any journeyman could have drafted it. Still, it has Walker's name to it, don't you see - it has Walker's name to it; that means everything."

"Is it cheaper than this would be," Tyrrel asked, for Le Neve had laid stress on the point that for economy of material, combined with strength of weight-resisting power, his own plan was remarkable.

"Cheaper!" Sir Edward echoed. "Oh dear, no. By no means. Nothing could very well be cheaper than this. There's genius in its construction, don't you see? It's a new idea, intelligently applied to the peculiarities and difficulties of a very unusual position, taking advantage most ingeniously of the natural support afforded by the rock and the inequalities of the situation; I should say your friend is well within the mark in the estimate he gives." He drummed his finger and calculated mentally. "It'd save the company from a hundred and fifty to two hundred thousand pounds, I fancy," he said, ruminating, after a minute.

"And do you mean to tell me," Tyrrel exclaimed, taken aback, "men of business like the directors of the Great North Midland will fling away two hundred thousand pounds of the shareholder's money as if it were dirt, by accepting Walker's plan when they might accept this one?"

Sir Edward opened his palms, like a Frenchman, in front of him. It was a trick he had picked up on foreign bourses.

"My dear fellow," he answered, compassionately, "directors are men, and to err is human. These great North Midland people are mere flesh and blood, and none of them very brilliant. They know Walker, and they'll be largely guided by Walker's advice in the matter. If he saw his way to make more out of contracting for carrying out somebody else's design, no doubt he'd do it. But failing that, he'll palm his own off upon them, and Stillingfleet'll accept it. You see with how little wisdom the railways of the world are governed! People think, if they get Walker to do a thing for them, they shift the responsibility upon Walker's shoulders. And knowing nothing themselves, they feel that's a great point; it saves them trouble and salves their consciences."

A new idea seemed to cross Tyrrel's mind. He leant

forward suddenly.

"But as to safety," he asked, with some anxiety, "viewed as a matter of life and death, I mean? Which of these two viaducts is likely to last longest, to be freest from danger, to give rise in the end to least and fewest accidents?"

"Why, your friend Le Neve's, of course," the millionaire answered, without a moment's hesitation.

"You think so?"

"I don't think so at all, my dear fellow, I know it. I'm sure of it. Look here," and he pulled out a design from a pigeon-hole in his desk; "this is in confidence, you understand. I oughtn't to show it to you; but I can trust your honor. Here's Walker's idea. It isn't an idea at all, in fact, it's just the ordinary old stone viaduct, with the ordinary dangers, and the ordinary iron girders - nothing in any way new or original. It's respectable mediocrity. On an affair like that, and with this awkward curve, too, just behind taking-off point, the liability to accident is considerably greater than in a construction like Le Neve's, where nothing's left to chance, and where every source of evil, such as land-springs, or freshets, or weakening, or concussion, is considered beforehand and successfully provided against. If a company only thought of the lives and limbs of its passengers - which it never does, of course - and had a head on its shoulders, which it seldom possesses, Le Neve's is undoubtedly the design it would adopt in the interests of security."

Tyrrel drew a long breath. "And you know all this," he said, "and yet you won't say a word for Le Neve to the directors. A recommendation from YOU, you see -"

Sir Edward shrugged his shoulders. "Impossible!" he answered, at once. "It would be a great breach of confidence. Remember, Walker showed me his design as a friend, and after having looked at it I couldn't go right off and say to Stillingfleet, 'I've seen Walker's plans, and also another fellow's, and I advise you, for my part, not to take my friend's.' It wouldn't be gentlemanly."

Tyrrel paused and reflected. He saw the dilemma. And yet, what was the breach of confidence or of etiquette to the deadly peril to life and limb involved in choosing the worst design instead of the better one? It was a hard nut to crack. He could see no way out of it.

"Besides," Sir Edward went on, musingly, "even if I told them they wouldn't believe me. Whatever Walker sends in they're sure to accept it. They've more confidence, I feel sure, in Walker than in anybody."

A light broke in on Walter Tyrrel's mind.

"Then the only way," he said, looking up, "would be ... to work upon Walker; induce him NOT to send in, if that can be managed."

"But it can't be," Sir Edward answered, with brisk promptitude. "Walker's a money-grubbing chap. If he sees a chance of making a few thousands more anywhere, depend upon it he'll make 'em. He's a martyr to money, he is. He toils and slaves for L. s. d. {money} all his life. He has no other interests."

"What can he want with it?" Tyrrel exclaimed. "He's a bachelor, isn't he, without wife or child? What can a man like that want to pile up filthy lucre for?"

"Can't say, I'm sure," Sir Edward answered, good humoredly. "I have my quiver full of them myself, and every guinea I get I find three of my children are quarreling among themselves for ten and sixpence apiece of it. But what Walker can want with money heaven only knows. If *I* were a bachelor, now, and had an estate of my own in Cornwall, say, or Devonshire, I'm sure I don't know what I'd do with my income."

Grant Allen

Tyrrel rose abruptly. The chance words had put an idea into his head.

"What's Walker's address?" he asked, in a very curt tone.

Sir Edward gave it him.

"You'll find him a tough nut, though," he added, with a smile, as he followed the enthusiastic young Cornishman to the door. "But I see you're in earnest. Good luck go with you!"

CHAPTER XII

A HARD BARGAIN

Tyrrel took a hansom, and tore round in hot haste to Erasmus Walker's house. He sent in his card. The famous engineer was happily at home. Tyrrel, all on fire, found himself ushered into the great man's study. Mr. Walker sat writing at a luxurious desk in a most luxurious room - writing, as if for dear life, in breathless haste and eagerness. He simply paused for a second in the midst of a sentence, and looked up impatiently at the intruder on his desperate hurry. Then he motioned Tyrrel into a chair with an imperious wave of his ivory penholder. After that, he went on writing for some moments in solemn silence. Only the sound of his steel nib, traveling fast as it could go over the foolscap sheet, broke for several seconds the embarrassing stillness.

Walter Tyrrel, therefore, had ample time meanwhile to consider his host and to take in his peculiarities before Walker had come to the end of his paragraph. The great engineer was a big-built, bull-necked, bullet-headed sort of person, with the self-satisfied air of monetary success, but with that ominous hardness about the corners of the mouth which constantly betrays the lucky man of business. His abundant long hair was iron-gray and wiry - Erasmus Walker had seldom time to waste in getting it cut - his eyes were small and shrewd; his hand was firm, and gripped the pen in its grasp like a ponderous crowbar. His writing, Tyrrel could see, was thick, black, and decisive. Altogether the kind of man on whose brow it was

Grant Allen

written in legible characters that it's dogged as does it. The delicately organized Cornishman felt an instinctive dislike at once for this great coarse mountain of a bullying Teuton. Yet for Cleer's sake he knew he mustn't rub him the wrong way. He must put up with Erasmus Walker and all his faults, and try to approach him by the most accessible side - if indeed any side were accessible at all, save the waistcoat pocket.

At last, however, the engineer paused a moment in his headlong course through sentence after sentence, held his pen half irresolute over a new blank sheet, and turning round to Tyrrel, without one word of apology, said, in a quick, decisive voice, "This is business, I suppose, business? for if not, I've no time. I'm very pressed this morning. Very pressed, indeed. Very pressed and occupied."

"Yes, it is business," Tyrrel answered, promptly, taking his cue with Celtic quickness. "Business that may be worth a good deal of money." Erasmus Walker pricked up his ears at that welcome sound, and let the pen drop quietly into the rack by his side. "Only I'm afraid I must ask for a quarter of an hour or so of your valuable time. You will not find it thrown away. You can name your own price for it."

"My dear sir," the engineer replied, taking up his visitor's card again and gazing at it hard with a certain inquiring scrutiny, "if it's business, and business of an important character, of course I need hardly say I'm very glad to attend to you. There are so many people who come bothering me for nothing, don't you know - charitable appeals or what not - that I'm obliged to make a hard and fast rule about interviews. But if it's business you mean, I'm your man at once. I live for public works. Go ahead. I'm all attention."

He wheeled round in his revolving chair, and faced Tyrrel in an attitude of sharp practical eagerness. His eye was all alert. It was clear, the man was keen on every passing chance of a stray hundred or two extra. His keenness disconcerted the conscientious and idealistic Cornishman. For a second or two

Tyrrel debated how to open fire upon so unwonted an enemy. At last he began, stammering, "I've a friend who has made a design for the Wharfedale Viaduct."

"Exactly," Erasmus Walker answered, pouncing down upon him like a hawk. "And I've made one too. And as mine's in the field, why, your friend's is waste paper."

His sharpness half silenced Tyrrel. But with an effort the younger man went on, in spite of interruption. "That's precisely what I've come about," he said; "I know that already. If only you'll have patience and hear me out while I unfold my plan, you'll find what I have to propose is all to your own interest. I'm prepared to pay well for the arrangement I ask. Will you name your own price for half an hour's conversation, and then listen to me straight on and without further interruption?"

Erasmus Walker glanced back at him with those keen ferret-like eyes of his. "Why, certainly," he answered; "I'll listen if you wish. We'll treat it as a consultation. My fees for consultation depend, of course, upon the nature of the subject on which advice is asked. But you'll pay well, you say, for the scheme you propose. Now, this is business. Therefore, we must be business-like. So first, what guarantee have I of your means and solvency? I don't deal with men of straw. Are you known in the City?" He jerked out his sentences as if words were extorted from him at so much per thousand.

"I am not," Tyrrel answered, quietly; "but I gave you my card, and you can see from it who I am - Walter Tyrrel of Penmorgan Manor. I'm a landed proprietor, with a good estate in Cornwall. And I'm prepared to risk - well, a large part of my property in the business I propose to you, without any corresponding risk on your part. In plain words, I'm prepared to pay you money down, if you will accede to my wish, on a pure matter of sentiment."

"Sentiment?" Mr. Walker replied, bringing his jaw down like a rat-trap, and gazing across at him, dubiously. "I don't deal in sentiment."

"No; probably not," Tyrrel answered. "But I said sentiment, Mr. Walker, and I'm willing to pay for it. I know very well it's an article at a discount in the City. Still, to me, it means money's worth, and I'm prepared to give money down to a good tune to humor it. Let me explain the situation. I'll do so as briefly and as simply as I can, if only you'll listen to me. A friend of mine, as I said, one Eustace Le Neve, who has been constructing engineer of the Rosario and Santa Fe, in the Argentine Confederacy, has made a design for the Wharfedale Viaduct. It's a very good design, and a practical design; and Sir Edward Jones, who has seen it, entirely approves of it."

"Jones is a good man," Mr. Walker murmured, nodding his head in acquiescence. "No dashed nonsense about Jones. Head screwed on the right way. Jones is a good man and knows what he's talking about." "Well, Jones says it's a good design," Tyrrel went on, breathing freer as he gauged his man more completely. "And the facts are just these: My friend's engaged to a young lady up in town here, in whom I take a deep interest - " Mr. Walker whistled low to himself, but didn't interrupt him - "a deep FRIENDLY interest," Tyrrel corrected, growing hot in the face at the man's evident insolent misconstruction of his motives; "and the long and the short of it is, his chance of marrying her depends very much upon whether or not he can get this design of his accepted by the directors."

"He can't," Mr. Walker said, promptly, "unless he buys me out. That's pat and flat. He can't, for mine's in; and mine's sure to be taken."

"So I understand," Tyrrel went on. "Your name, I'm told, carries everything before it. But what I want to suggest now is simply this - How much will you take, money down on the nail, this minute, to withdraw your own design from the informal competition?"

Erasmus Walker gasped hard, drew a long breath, and stared at him. "How much will I take," he repeated, slowly; "how - much - will - I - take - to withdraw my design? Well, that IS remarkable!"

"I mean it," Tyrrel repeated, with a very serious face. "This is to me, I will confess, a matter of life and death. I want to see my friend Le Neve in a good position in the world, such as his talents entitle him to. I don't care how much I spend in order to insure it. So what I want to know is just this and nothing else - how much will you take to withdraw from the competition?"

Erasmus Walker laid his two hands on his fat knees, with his legs wide open, and stared long and hard at his incomprehensible visitor. So strange a request stunned for a moment even that sound business head. A minute or two he paused. Then, with a violent effort, he pulled himself together. "Come, come," he said, "Mr. Tyrrel; let's be practical and above-board. I don't want to rob you. I don't want to plunder you. I see you mean business. But how do you know, suppose even you buy me out, this young fellow's design has any chance of being accepted? What reason have you to think the Great North Midland people are likely to give such a job to an unknown beginner?"

"Sir Edward Jones says it's admirable," Tyrrel ventured, dubiously.

"Sir Edward Jones says it's admirable! Well, that's good, as far as it goes. Jones knows what he's talking about. Head's screwed on the right way. But has your friend any interest with the directors - that's the question? Have you reason to think, if he sends it in, and I hold back mine, his is the plan they'd be likely to pitch upon?"

"I go upon its merits," Walter Tyrrel said, quietly.

"The very worst thing on earth any man can ever possibly go

upon," the man of business retorted, with cynical confidence. "If that's all you've got to say, my dear sir, it wouldn't be fair of me to make money terms with you. I won't discuss my price in the matter till I've some reason to believe this idea of yours is workable."

"I have the designs here all ready," Walter Tyrrel replied, holding them out. "Plans, elevations, specifications, estimates, sections, figures, everything. Will you do me the favor to look at them? Then, perhaps, you'll be able to see whether or not the offer's genuine."

The great engineer took the roll with a smile. He opened it hastily, in a most skeptical humor. Walter Tyrrel leant over him, and tried just at first to put in a word or two of explanation, such as Le Neve had made to himself; but an occasionally testy "Yes, yes; I see," was all the thanks he got for his pains and trouble. After a minute or two he found out it was better to let the engineer alone. That practiced eye picked out in a moment the strong and weak points of the whole conception. Gradually, however, as Walker went on, Walter Tyrrel could see he paid more and more attention to every tiny detail. His whole manner altered. The skeptical smile faded away, little by little, from those thick, sensuous lips, and a look of keen interest took its place by degrees on the man's eager features. "That's good!" he murmured more than once, as he examined more closely some section or enlargement. "That's good! very good! knows what he's about, this Eustace Le Neve man!" Now and again he turned back, to re-examine some special point. "Clever dodge!" he murmured, half to himself. "Clever dodge, undoubtedly. Make an engineer in time - no doubt at all about that - if only they'll give him his head, and not try to thwart him."

Tyrrel waited till he'd finished. Then he leant forward once more. "Well, what do you think of it now?" he asked, flushing hot. "Is this business - or otherwise?"

"Oh, business, business," the great engineer murmured,

musically, regarding the papers before him with a certain professional affection. "It's a devilish clever plan - I won't deny that - and it's devilish well carried out in every detail."

Tyrrel seized his opportunity. "And if you were to withdraw your own design," he asked, somewhat nervously, hardly knowing how best to frame his delicate question, "do you think ... the directors ... would be likely to accept this one?"

Erasmus Walker hummed and hawed. He twirled his fat thumbs round one another in doubt. Then he answered oracularly, "They might, of course; and yet, again, they mightn't."

"Upon whom would the decision rest?" Tyrrel inquired, looking hard at him.

"Upon me, almost entirely," the great engineer responded at once, with cheerful frankness. "To say the plain truth, they've no minds of their own, these men. They'd ask my advice, and accept it implicitly."

"So Jones told me," Tyrrel answered.

"So Jones told you - quite right," the engineer echoed, with a complacent nod. "They've no minds of their own, you see. They'll do just as I tell them."

"And you think this design of Le Neve's a good one, both mechanically and financially, and also exceptionally safe as regards the lives and limbs of passengers and employees?" Tyrrel inquired once more, with anxious particularity. His tender conscience made him afraid to do anything in the matter unless he was quite sure in his own mind he was doing no wrong in any way either to shareholders, competitors, or the public generally.

"My dear sir," Mr. Walker replied, fingering the papers lovingly, "it's an admirable design - sound, cheap, and practical. It's as good as it can be. To tell you the truth, I admire it immensely."

"Well, then," Tyrrel said at last, all his scruples removed - "let's come to business. I put it plainly. How much will you take to withdraw your own design, and to throw your weight into the scale in favor of my friend's here?"

Erasmus Walker closed one eye, and rewarded his visitor fixedly out of the other for a minute or two in silence, as if taking his bearings. It was a trick he had acquired from frequent use of a theodolite. Then he answered at last, after a long, deep pause, "It's YOUR deal, Mr. Tyrrel. Make me an offer, won't you?"

"Five thousand pounds?" tremblingly suggested Walter Tyrrel.

Erasmus Walker opened his eye slowly, and never allowed his surprise to be visible on his face. Why, to him, a job like that, entailing loss of time in personal supervision, was hardly worth three. The plans were perfunctory, and as far as there was anything in them, could be used again elsewhere. He could employ his precious days meanwhile to better purpose in some more showy and profitable work than this half-hatched viaduct. But this was an upset price. "Not enough," he murmured, slowly, shaking his bullet head. "It's a fortune to the young man. You must make a better offer."

Walter Tyrrel's lip quivered. "Six thousand," he said, promptly.

The engineer judged from the promptitude of the reply that the Cornish landlord must still be well squeezable. He shook his head gain. "No, no; not enough," he answered short. "Not enough - by a long way."

"Eight," Tyrrel suggested, drawing a deep breath of suspense. It was a big sum, indeed, for a modest estate like Penmorgan.

The engineer shook his head once more. That rush up two thousand at once was a very good feature. The man who could mount by two thousand at a time might surely be squeezed to the even figure.

"I'm afraid," Walter said, quivering, after a brief mental calculation - mortgage at four per cent - and agricultural depression running down the current value of land in the market - "I couldn't by any possibility go beyond ten thousand. But to save my friend - and to get the young lady married - I wouldn't mind going as far as that to meet you."

The engineer saw at once, with true business instinct, his man had reached the end of his tether. He struck while the iron was hot and clinched the bargain. "Well, - as there's a lady in the case" - he said, gallantly, - "and to serve a young man of undoubted talent, who'll do honor to the profession, I don't mind closing with you. I'll take ten thousand, money down, to back out of it myself, and I'll say what I can - honestly - to the Midland Board in your friend's favor."

"Very good," Tyrrel answered, drawing a deep breath of relief. "I ask no more than that. Say what you can honestly. The money shall be paid you before the end of a fortnight."

"Only, mind," Mr. Walker added in an impressive after-thought, "I can't, of course, ENGAGE that the Great North Midland people will take my advice. You mustn't come down upon me for restitution and all that if your friend don't succeed and they take some other fellow. All I guarantee for certain is to withdraw my own plans - not to send in anything myself for the competition."

"I fully understand," Tyrrel answered. "And I'm content to risk it. But, mind, if any other design is submitted of superior excellence to Le Neve's, I wouldn't wish you on any account to - to do or say anything that goes against your conscience."

Erasmus Walker stared at him. "What - after paying ten

thousand pounds?" he said, "to secure the job?"

Tyrrel nodded a solemn nod. "Especially," he added, "if you think it safer to life and limb. I should never forgive myself if an accident were to occur on Eustace Le Neve's viaduct."

CHAPTER XIII

ANGEL AND DEVIL

Tyrrel left Erasmus Walker's house that morning in a turmoil of mingled exultation and fear. At least he had done his best to atone for the awful results of his boyish act of criminal thoughtlessness. He had tried to make it possible for Cleer to marry Eustace, and thereby to render the Trevennacks happier in their sonless old age; and what was more satisfactory still, he had crippled himself in doing it. There was comfort even in that. Expiation, reparation! He wouldn't have cared for the sacrifice so much if it had cost him less. But it would cost him dear indeed. He must set to work at once now and raise the needful sum by mortgaging Penmorgan up to the hilt to do it.

After all, of course, the directors might choose some other design than Eustace's. But he had done what he could. And he would hope for the best, at any rate. For Cleer's sake, if the worst came, he would have risked and lost much. While if Cleer's life was made happy, he would be happy in the thought of it.

He hailed another hansom, and drove off, still on fire, to his lawyer's in Victoria Street. On the way, he had to go near Paddington Station. He didn't observe, as he did so, a four-wheel cab that passed him with luggage on top, from Ivybridge to London. It was the Trevennacks, just returned from their holiday on Dartmoor. But Michael Trevennack had seen him; and his brow grew suddenly dark. He pinched his nails into his

Grant Allen

palm at sight of that hateful creature, though not a sound escaped him; for Cleer was in the carriage, and the man was Eustace's friend. Trevennack accepted Eustace perforce, after that night on Michael's Crag; for he knew it was politic; and indeed, he liked the young man himself well enough - there was nothing against him after all, beyond his friendship with Tyrrel; but had it not been for the need for avoiding scandal after the adventure on the rock, he would never have allowed Cleer to speak one word to any friend or acquaintance of her brother's murderer.

As it was, however, he never alluded to Tyrrel in any way before Cleer. He had learnt to hold his tongue. Madman though he was, he knew when to be silent.

That evening at home, Cleer had a visit from Eustace, who came round to tell her how Tyrrel had been to see the great engineer, Erasmus Walker; and how it was all a mistake that Walker was going to send in plans for the Wharfedale Viaduct - nay, how the big man had approved of his own design, and promised to give it all the support in his power. For Tyrrel was really an awfully kind friend, who had pushed things for him like a brick, and deserved the very best they could both of them say about him.

But of course Eustace hadn't the faintest idea himself by what manner of persuasion Walter Tyrrel had commended his friend's designs to Erasmus Walker. If he had, needless to say, he would never have accepted the strange arrangement.

"And now, Cleer," Eustace cried, jubilant and radiant with the easy confidence of youth and love, "I do believe I shall carry the field at last, and spring at a bound into a first-rate position among engineers in England."

"And then?" Cleer asked, nestling close to his side.

"And then," Eustace went on, smiling tacitly at her native simplicity, "as it would mean permanent work in superintending and so forth, I see no reason why - we shouldn't get married immediately."

They were alone in the breakfast room, where Mrs. Trevennack had left them. They were alone, like lovers. But in the drawing-room hard by, Trevennack himself was saying to his wife with a face of suppressed excitement, "I saw him again to-day, Lucy. I saw him again, that devil - in a hansom near Paddington. If he stops in town, I'm sure I don't know what I'm ever to do. I came back from Devonshire, having fought the devil hard, as I thought, and conquered him. I felt I'd got him under. I felt he was no match for me. But when I see that man's face the devil springs up at me again in full force, and grapples with me. Is he Satan himself? I believe he must be. For I feel I must rush at him and trample him under foot, as I trampled him long ago on the summit of Niphates."

In a tremor of alarm Mrs. Trevennack held his hand. Oh, what would she ever do if the outbreak came ... before Cleer was married! She could see the constant strain of holding himself back was growing daily more and more difficult for her unhappy husband. Indeed, she couldn't bear it herself much longer. If Cleer didn't marry soon, Michael would break out openly - perhaps would try to murder that poor man Tyrrel - and then Eustace would be afraid, and all would be up with them.

By and by, Eustace came in to tell them the good news. He said nothing about Tyrrel, at least by name, lest he should hurt Trevennack; he merely mentioned that a friend of his had seen Erasmus Walker that day, and that Walker had held out great hopes of success for him in this Wharfedale Viaduct business. Trevennack listened with a strange mixture of interest and contempt. He was glad the young man was likely to get on in his chosen profession - for Cleer's sake, if it would enable them to marry. But, oh, what a fuss it seemed to him to make about such a trifle as a mere bit of a valley that one could fly across in a second - to him who could become

". . . to his proper shape returned
A seraph winged: six wings he wore, to shade
His lineaments divine; the pair that clad
Each shoulder broad, came mantling o'er his breast
With regal ornament; the middle pair
Girt like a starry zone his waist, and round
Skirted his loins and thighs, the third his feet
Shadowed from either heel with feathered mail."

And then they talked to HIM about the difficulties of building a few hundred yards of iron bridge across a miserable valley! Why, was it not he and his kind of whom it was written that they came

"Gliding through the even
On a sunbeam, swift as a shooting star
In autumn thwarts the night?"

A viaduct indeed! a paltry human viaduct! What need, with such as him, to talk of bridges or viaducts?

As Eustace left that evening, Mrs. Trevennack followed him out, and beckoned him mysteriously into the dining-room at the side for a minute's conversation. The young man followed her, much wondering what this strange move could mean. Mrs. Trevennack fell back, half faint, into a chair, and gazed at him with a frightened look very rare on that brave face of hers. "Oh, Eustace," she said, hurriedly, "do you know what's happened? Mr. Tyrrel's in town. Michael saw him to-day. He was driving near Paddington. Now do you think... you could do anything to keep him out of Michael's way? I dread their meeting. I don't know whether you know it, but Michael has some grudge against him. For Cleer's sake and for yours, do keep them apart, I beg of you. If they meet, I can't answer for what harm may come of it."

Eustace was taken aback at her unexpected words. Not even to Cleer had he ever hinted in any way at the strange disclosure Walter Tyrrel made to him that first day at Penmorgan. He hesitated how to answer her without betraying his friend's secret. At last he said, as calmly as he could, "I guessed, to tell you the truth, there was some cause of quarrel. I'll do my very best to keep Tyrrel out of the way, Mrs. Trevennack, as you wish it. But I'm afraid he won't be going down from town for some time to come, for he told me only to-day he had business at his lawyer's, in Victoria Street, Westminster, which might keep him here a fortnight. Indeed, I rather doubt whether he'll care to go down again until he knows for certain, one way or the other, about the Wharfedale Viaduct."

Mrs. Trevennack sank back in her chair, very pale and wan. "Oh, what shall we do if they meet?" she cried, wringing her hands in despair. "What shall we do if they meet? This is more than I can endure. Eustace, Eustace, I shall break down. My burden's too heavy for me!"

The young man leant over her like a son. "Mrs. Trevennack," he said, gently, smoothing her silvery white hair with sympathetic fingers, "I think I can keep them apart. I'll speak seriously to Tyrrel about it. He's a very good fellow, and he'll do anything I ask of him. I'm sure he'll try to avoid falling in with your husband. He's my kindest of friends; and he'd cut off his hand to serve me."

One word of sympathy brought tears into Mrs. Trevennack's eyes. She looked up through them, and took the young man's hand in hers. "It was HE who spoke to Erasmus Walker, I suppose," she murmured, slowly.

And Eustace, nodding assent, answered in a low voice, "It was he, Mrs. Trevennack. He's a dear good fellow."

The orphaned mother clasped her hands. This was too, too much. And Michael, if the fit came upon him, would strangle that young man, who was doing his best after all for Cleer and Eustace!

But that night in his bed Trevennack lay awake, chuckling

grimly to himself in an access of mad triumph. He fancied he was fighting his familiar foe, on a tall Cornish peak, in archangelic fashion; and he had vanquished his enemy, and was trampling on him furiously. But the face of the fallen seraph was not the face of Michael Angelo's Satan, as he oftenest figured it - for Michael Angelo, his namesake, was one of Trevennack's very chiefest admirations; - it was the face of Walter Tyrrel, who killed his dear boy, writhing horribly in the dust, and crying for mercy beneath him.

CHAPTER XIV

AT ARM'S LENGTH

For three or four weeks Walter Tyrrel remained in town, awaiting the result of the Wharfedale Viaduct competition. With some difficulty he raised and paid over meanwhile to Erasmus Walker the ten thousand pounds of blackmail - for it was little else - agreed upon between them. The great engineer accepted the money with as little compunction as men who earn large incomes always display in taking payment for doing nothing. It is an enviable state of mind, unattainable by most of us who work hard for our living. He pocketed his check with a smile, as if it were quite in the nature of things that ten thousand pounds should drop upon him from the clouds without rhyme or reason. To Tyrrel, on the other hand, with his sensitive conscience, the man's greed and callousness seemed simply incomprehensible. He stood aghast at such sharp practice. But for Cleer's sake, and to ease his own soul, he paid it all over without a single murmur.

And then the question came up in his mind, "Would it be effectual after all? Would Walker play him false? Would he throw the weight of his influence into somebody else's scale? Would the directors submit as tamely as he thought to his direction or dictation?" It would be hard on Tyrrel if, after his spending ten thousand pounds without security of any sort, Eustace were to miss the chance, and Cleer to go unmarried.

At the end of a month, however, as Tyrrel sat one morning in his own room at the Metropole, which he mostly frequented, Eustace Le Neve rushed in, full of intense excitement. Tyrrel's heart rose in his mouth. He grew pale with agitation. The question had been decided one way or the other he saw.

"Well; which is it?" he gasped out. "Hit or miss? Have you got it?"

"Yes; I've got it!" Eustace answered, half beside himself with delight. "I've got it! I've got it! The chairman and Walker have just been round to call on me, and congratulate me on my success. Walker says my fortune's made. It's a magnificent design. And in any case it'll mean work for me for the next four years; after which I'll not want for occupation elsewhere. So now, of course, I can marry almost immediately."

"Thank God!" Tyrrel murmured, falling back into his chair as he spoke, and turning deadly white.

He was glad of it, oh, so glad; and yet, in his own heart, it would cost him many pangs to see Cleer really married in good earnest to Eustace.

He had worked for it with all his might to be sure; he had worked for it and paid for it! and now he saw his wishes on the very eve of fulfillment, the natural man within him rose up in revolt against the complete success of his own unselfish action.

As for Mrs. Trevennack, when she heard the good news, she almost fainted with joy. It might yet be in time. Cleer might be married now before poor Michael broke forth in that inevitable paroxysm.

For inevitable she felt it was at last. As each day went by it grew harder and harder for the man to contain himself. Fighting desperately against it every hour, immersing himself as much as he could in the petty fiddling details of the office and the Victualing Yard so as to keep the fierce impulse under due control, Michael Trevennack yet found the mad mood within him more and more ungovernable with each week that went by. As he put it to his own mind he could feel his wings growing as if they must burst through the skin; he could feel it harder and ever harder as time went on to conceal the truth, to pretend he was a mere man, when he knew himself to be really the Prince of the Archangels, to busy himself about contracts for pork, and cheese, and biscuits, when he could wing his way n boldly over sea and land, or stand forth before the world in gorgeous gear, armed as of yore in the adamant and gold of his celestial panoply!

So Michael Trevennack thought in his own seething soul. But that strong, brave woman, his wife, bearing her burden unaided, and watching him closely day and night with a keen eye of mingled love and fear, could see that the madness was gaining on him gradually. Oftener and oftener now did he lose himself in his imagined world; less and less did he tread the solid earth beneath us. Mrs. Trevennack had by this time but one anxious care left in life - to push on as fast as possible Cleer and Eustace's marriage.

But difficulties intervened, as they always WILL intervene in this work-a-day world of ours. First of all there were formalities about the appointment itself. Then, even when all was arranged, Eustace found he had to go north in person, shortly after Christmas, and set to work with a will at putting his plan into practical shape for contractor and workmen. And as soon as he got there he saw at once he must stick at it for six months at least before he could venture to take a short holiday for the sake of getting married. Engineering is a very absorbing trade; it keeps a man day and night at the scene of his labors.

Storm or flood at any moment may ruin everything. It would be prudent too, Eustace thought, to have laid by a little more for household expenses, before plunging into the unknown sea of matrimony; and though Mrs. Trevennack, flying full in the face of all matronly respect for foresight in young people, urged him constantly to marry, money or no money, and never mind about a honeymoon, Eustace stuck to his point and determined to take no decisive step till he saw how the work was turning out in Wharfedale. It was thus full August of the succeeding year before he could fix a date definitely; and then, to Cleer's great joy, he named a day at last, about the beginning of September.

It was an immense relief to Mrs. Trevennack's mind when, after one or two alterations, she knew the third was finally fixed upon. She had good reasons of her own for wishing it to be early; for the twenty-ninth is Michaelmas Day, and it was always with difficulty that her husband could be prevented from breaking out before the eyes of the world on that namesake feast of St. Michael and All Angels. For, on that sacred day, when in every Church in Christendom his importance as the generalissimo of the angelic host was remembered and commemorated, it seemed hard indeed to the seraph in disguise that he must still guard his incognito, still go on as usual with his petty higgling over corned beef and biscuits and the price of jute sacking. "There was war in heaven," said the gospel for the day - that sonorous gospel Mrs. Trevennack so cordially dreaded - for her husband would always go to church at morning service, and hold himself more erect than was his wont, to hear it - "There was war in heaven; Michael and his angels fought against the dragon; and the dragon fought and his angels, and prevailed not." And should he, who could thus battle against all the powers of evil, be held in check any longer, as with a leash of straw, by the Lords Commissioners of the Admiralty? No, no, he would stand forth in his true angelic shape, and show these martinets what form they had ignorantly taken for mere Michael Trevennack of the Victualing Department!

One thing alone eased Mrs. Trevennack's mind through all those weary months of waiting and watching: Walter Tyrrel had long since gone back again to Penmorgan. Her husband had been free from that greatest of all temptations, to a mad paroxysm of rage - the sight of the man who, as he truly believed, had killed their Michael. And now, if only Tyrrel would keep away from town till Cleer was married and all was settled - Mrs. Trevennack sighed deep - she would almost count herself a happy woman!

On the day of Cleer's wedding, however, Walter Tyrrel came to town. He came on purpose. He couldn't resist the temptation of seeing with his own eyes the final success of his general plan, even though it cost him the pang of watching the marriage of the one girl he ever truly loved to another man by his own deliberate contrivance. But he didn't forget Eustace Le Neve's earnest warning, that he should keep out of the way of Michael Trevennack. Even without Eustace, his own conscience would have urged that upon him. The constant burden of his remorse for that boyish crime weighed hard upon him every hour of every day that he lived. He didn't dare on such a morning to face the father of the boy he had unwittingly and half-innocently murdered.

So, very early, as soon as the church was opened, he stole in unobserved, and took a place by himself in the farthest corner of the gallery. A pillar concealed him from view; for further security he held his handkerchief constantly in front of his face, or shielded himself behind one of the big free-seat prayer-books. Cleer came in looking beautiful in her wedding dress; Mrs. Trevennack's pathetic face glowed radiant for once in this final realization of her dearest wishes. A single second only, near the end of the ceremony, Tyrrel leaned forward incautiously, anxious to see Cleer at an important point of the proceedings. At the very same instant Trevennack raised his face. Their eyes met in a flash. Tyrrel drew back, horrorstruck, and penitent at his own intrusion at such a critical moment. But, strange to say, Trevennack took no overt notice. Had his wife only known she would have sunk in her seat in her agony of fear. But happily she didn't know. Trevennack went through the ceremony, all outwardly calm; he gave no sign of what he had seen, even to his wife herself. He buried it deep in his own heart. That made it all the more dangerous.

CHAPTER XV

ST. MICHAEL DOES BATTLE

The wedding breakfast went off pleasantly, without a hitch of any sort. Trevennack, always dignified and always a grand seigneur, rose to the occasion with his happiest spirit. The silver-haired wife, gazing up at him, felt proud of him as of old, and was for once quite at her ease. For all was over now, thank heaven, and dear Cleer was married!

That same afternoon the bride and bridegroom started off for their honeymoon to the Tyrol and Italy. When Mrs. Trevennack was left alone with her husband it was with a thankful heart. She turned to him, flowing over in soul with joy. "Oh, Michael," she cried, melting, "I'm so happy, so happy, so happy."

Trevennack stooped down and kissed her forehead tenderly. He had always been a good husband, and he loved her with all his heart. "That's well, Lucy," he answered. "Thank God, it's all over. For I can't hold out much longer. The strain's too much for me." He paused a moment, and looked at her. "Lucy," he said, once more, clasping his forehead with one hand, "I've fought against it hard. I'm fighting against it still. But at times it almost gets the better of me. Do you know who I saw in the church this morning, skulking behind a pillar? - that man Walter Tyrrel."

Mrs. Trevennack gazed at him all aghast. This was surely a

delusion, a fixed idea, an insane hallucination. "Oh, no, dear," she cried, prying deep into his eyes. "It couldn't be he, it couldn't. You must be mistaken, Michael. I'm sure he's not in London."

"No more mistaken than I am this minute," Trevennack answered, rushing over to the window, and pointing with one hand eagerly. "See, see! there he is, Lucy - the man that killed our poor, dear Michael!"

Mrs. Trevennack uttered a little cry, half sob, half wail, as she looked out of the window and, under the gas-lamps opposite, recognized through the mist the form of Walter Tyrrel.

But Trevennack didn't rush out at him as she feared and believed he would. He only stood still in his place and glared at his enemy. "Not now," he said, slowly; "not now, on Cleer's wedding day. But some other time - more suitable. I hear it in my ears; I hear the voice still ringing: 'Go, Michael, of celestial armies prince!' I can't disobey. I shall go in due time. I shall fight the enemy."

And he sank back in his chair, with his eyes staring wildly.

For the next week or two, while Cleer wrote home happy letters from Paris, Innsbruck, Milan, Venice, Florence, poor Mrs. Trevennack was tortured inwardly with another terrible doubt; had Michael's state become so dangerous at last that he must be put under restraint as a measure of public security? For Walter Tyrrel's sake, ought she to make his condition known to the world at large - and spoil Cleer's honeymoon? She shrank from that final necessity with a deadly shrinking. Day after day she put the discovery off, and solaced her soul with the best intentions - as what true woman would not?

But we know where good intentions go. On the morning of the twenty-ninth, which is Michaelmas Day, the poor mother rose in fear and trembling. Michael, to all outward appearance, was as sane as usual. He breakfasted and went down to the

Grant Allen

office, as was his wont.

When he arrived there, however, he found letters from Falmouth awaiting him with bad news. His presence was needed at once. He must miss his projected visit to St. Michael's, Cornhill. He must go down to Cornwall.

Hailing a cab at the door he hastened back to Paddington just in time for the Cornish express. This was surely a call. The words rang in his ears louder and clearer than ever, "Go, Michael, of celestial armies prince!" He would go and obey them. He would trample under foot this foul fiend that masqueraded in human shape as his dear boy's murderer. He would wield once more that huge two-handed sword, brandished aloft, wide-wasting, in unearthly warfare. He would come out in his true shape before heaven and earth as the chief of the archangels.

Stepping into a first-class compartment he found himself, unluckily for his present mood, alone. All the way down to Exeter the fit was on him. He stood up in the carriage, swaying his unseen blade, celestial temper fine, and rolling forth in a loud voice Miltonic verses of his old encounters in heaven with the powers of darkness.

"Now waved their fiery swords, and in the air
Made horrid circles; two broad suns their shields
Blazed opposite, while expectation stood
In horror."

He mouthed out the lines in a perfect ecstasy of madness. It was delightful to be alone. He could give his soul full vent. He knew he was mad. He knew he was an archangel.

And all the way down he repeated to himself, many times over, that he would trample under foot that base fiend Walter Tyrrel. Satan has many disguises; squat like a toad, close at the ear of Eve, he sat in Paradise; for

"...spirits as they please
Can limb themselves, and color, or size assume
As likes them best, condense or rare."

If he himself, Michael, prince of celestial hosts, could fit his angelic majesty to the likeness of a man, Trevennack - could not Satan meet him on his own ground, and try to thwart him as of old in the likeness of a man, Walter Tyrrel - his dear boy's murderer.

As far as Exeter this was his one train of thought. But from there to Plymouth new passengers got in. They turned the current. Trevennack changed his mind rapidly. Another mood came over him. His wife's words struck him vaguely in some tenderer place. "Fight the devil WITHIN you, Michael. Fight him there, and conquer him." That surely was fitter far for an angelic nature. That foeman was worthier his celestial steel. "Turn homeward, angel, now, and melt with ruth!" Not his to do vengeance on the man Walter Tyrrel. Not his to play the divine part of vindicator. In his madness even Trevennack was magnanimous. Leave the creature to the torment of his own guilty soul. Do angels care for thrusts of such as he? Tantaene animis coelestibus irae?

At Ivybridge station the train slowed, and then stopped. Trevennack, accustomed to the Cornish express, noted the stoppage with surprise. "We're not down to pull up here!" he said, quickly, to the guard.

"No sir," the guard answered, touching his hat with marked respect, for he knew the Admiralty official well. "Signals are against us. Line's blocked as far as Plymouth."

"I'll get out here, then," Trevennack said, in haste; and the guard opened the door. A new idea had rushed suddenly into the madman's head. This was St. Michael's Day - his own day; and there was St. Michael's Tor - his own tor - full in sight before him. He would go up there this very evening, and before the eyes of all the world, in his celestial armor, taking

Grant Allen

Lucy's advice, do battle with and quell this fierce devil within him.

No sooner thought than done. Fiery hot within, he turned out of the gate, and as the shades of autumn evening began to fall, walked swiftly up the moor toward the tor and the uplands.

As he walked his heart beat to a lilting rhythm within him. "Go, Michael, of celestial armies prince! - Go, Michael! - Go, Michael! Go, Michael, of celestial armies prince - Go, Michael! - Go, Michael!"

The moor was draped in fog. It was a still, damp evening. Swirling clouds rose slowly up, and lifted at times and disclosed the peaty hollows, the high tors, the dusky heather. But Trevennack stumbled on, o'er bog or steep, through strait, rough, dense, or rare, as chance might lead him, clambering ever toward his goal, now seen, now invisible - the great stack of wild rock that crowned the gray undulating moor to northward. Often he missed his way; often he floundered for awhile in deep ochreous bottoms, up to his knees in soft slush, but with some strange mad instinct he wandered on nevertheless, and slowly drew near the high point he was aiming at.

By this time it was pitch dark. The sun had set and fog obscured the starlight. But Trevennack, all on fire, wandered madly forward and scaled the rocky tor by the well-known path, guided not by sight, but by pure instinctive groping. In his present exalted state, indeed, he had no need of eyes. What matters earthly darkness to angelic feet? He could pick his own way through the gloom, though all the fiends from hell in serried phalanx broke loose to thwart him. He would reach the top at last; reach the top; reach the top, and there fight that old serpent who lay in wait to destroy him. At last he gained the peak, and stood with feet firmly planted on the little rocky platform. Now, Satan, come on! Ha, traitor, come, if you dare! Your antagonist is ready for you!

Cr'r'r'k! as he stood there, waiting, a terrible shock brought him to himself all at once with startling suddenness. Trevennack drew back aghast and appalled. Even in his mad exaltation this strange assault astonished him. He had expected a struggle, indeed; he had expected a conflict, but with a spiritual foe; to meet his adversary in so bodily a form as this, wholly startled and surprised him. For it was a fierce earthly shock he received upon his right leg as he mounted the rocky platform. Satan had been lying in wait for him then, expecting him, waylaying him, and in corporeal presence too. For this was a spear of good steel! This was a solid Thing that assaulted him as he rose - assaulted him with frantic rage and uncontrollable fury!

For a moment Trevennack was stunned - the sharpness of the pain and the suddenness of the attack took both breath and sense away from him. He stood there one instant, irresolute, before he knew how to comport himself. But before he could make up his mind - cr'r'k, a second time - the Presence had assailed him again, fighting with deadly force, and in a white heat of frenzy. Trevennack had no leisure to think what this portent might mean. Man or fiend, it was a life-and-death struggle now between them. He stood face to face at last in mortal conflict with his materialized enemy. What form the Evil Thing had assumed to suit his present purpose Trevennack knew not, nor did he even care. Stung with pain and terror he rushed forward blindly upon his enraged assailant, and closed with him at once, tooth and nail, in a deadly grapple.

A more terrible battle man and brute never fought. Trevennack had no sword, no celestial panoply. But he could wrestle like a Cornishman. He must trample his foe under foot, then, in this final struggle, by sheer force of strong thews and strained muscles alone. He fought the Creature as it stood, flinging his arms round it wildly. The Thing seemed to rear itself as if on cloven hoofs. Trevennack seized it round the waist, and grasping it hard in an iron grip, clung to it with all the wild energy of madness. Yield, Satan, yield! But still the Creature eluded him. Once more it drew back a pace - he felt its hot breath, he smelt its hateful smell - and prepared to rush again at him. Trevennack bent down to receive its attack, crouching. The Creature burst full tilt on him - it almost threw him over. Trevennack caught it in his horror and awe - caught it bodily by the horns - for horned it seemed to be, as well as cloven-footed - and by sheer force of arm held it off from him an elbow's length one minute. The Thing struggled and reared again. Yes, yes, it was Satan - he felt him all over now - a devil undisguised - but Satan rather in medieval than in Miltonic fashion. His skin was rough and hairy as a satyr's; his odor was foul; his feet were cleft; his horns sharp and terrible. He flung him from him horrified.

Quick as lightning the demon rose again, and tilted fiercely at him once more. It was a death fight between those two for that rocky platform. Should Satan thus usurp St. Michael's Tor? Ten thousand times, no! Yield, yield! No surrender! Each knew the ground well, and even in the dark and in the mad heat of the conflict, each carefully avoided the steep edge of the precipice. But the fiend knew it best, apparently. He had been lying in a snug nook, under lee of a big rock, sharpening his sword on its side, before Trevennack came up there. Against this rock he took his stand, firm as a rock himself, and seemed to defy his enemy's arms to dislodge him from his position.

Trevennack's hands and legs were streaming now with blood. His left arm was sorely wounded. His thumb hung useless. But with the strange energy of madness he continued the desperate conflict against his unseen foe. Never should Michael turn and yield to the deadly assaults of the Evil One! He rushed on blindly once more, and the Adversary stooped to oppose him. Again, a terrible shock, it almost broke both his knees; but by sheer strength of nerve he withstood it, still struggling. Then they closed in a final grapple. It was a tooth-and-nail conflict. They fought one another with every weapon they possessed; each hugged each in their fury; they tilted, and tore, and wrestled, and bit, and butted.

Trevennack's coat was in ribbons, his arm was ripped and

bleeding; but he grasped the Adversary still, he fought blindly to the end. Down, Satan, I defy thee!

It was a long, fierce fight! At last, bit by bit, the Enemy began to yield. Trevennack had dashed him against the crag time after time like a log, till he too was torn and hurt and bleeding. His flesh was like pulp. He could endure the unequal fight no longer. He staggered and gave way. A great joy rose up tremulous in Trevennack's heart. Even without his celestial sword, then, he had vanquished his enemy. He seized the Creature round the middle, dragged it, a dead weight, in his weary arms, to the edge of the precipice, and dropped it, feebly resisting, on to the bare rock beneath him.

Victory! Victory! Once more, a great victory!

He stood on the brink of the tor, and poised himself, as if for flight, in his accustomed attitude. But he was faint from loss of blood, and his limbs shook under him.

A light seemed to break before his blinded eyes. Victory! Victory! It was the light from heaven! He stared forward to welcome it. The brink of the precipice? What was THAT to such as he? He would spread his wings - for once - at last - thus! thus! and fly forward on full pinions to his expected triumph!

He raised both arms above his head, and spread them out as if for flight. His knees trembled fearfully. His fingers quivered. Then he launched himself on the air and fell. His eyes closed half-way. He lost consciousness. He fainted. Before he had reached the bottom he was wholly insensible.

Next day it was known before noon in London that a strange and inexplicable accident had befallen Mr. Michael Trevennack C.M.G., the well-known Admiralty official, on the moor near Ivybridge. Mr. Trevennack, it seemed, had started by the Cornish express for Falmouth, on official business; but the line being blocked between Ivybridge and

Plymouth, he had changed his plans and set out to walk, as was conjectured, by a devious path across the moor to Tavistock. Deceased knew the neighborhood well, and was an enthusiastic admirer of its tors and uplands. But fog coming on, the unfortunate gentleman, it was believed, had lost his way, and tried to shelter himself for a time behind a tall peak of rock which he used frequently to visit during his summer holidays. There he was apparently attacked by a savage moorland ram - one of that wild breed of mountain sheep peculiar to Dartmoor, and famous for the strength and ferocity often displayed by the fathers of the flock. Mr. Trevennack was unarmed, and a terrible fight appeared to have taken place between these ill-matched antagonists on the summit of the rocks, full details of which, the Telegram said in its curt business-like way, were too ghastly for publication. After a long and exhausting struggle, however, the combatants must either have slipped on the wet surface and tumbled over the edge of the rocks together in a deadly grapple, or else, as seemed more probable from the positions in which the bodies were found, the unhappy gentleman had just succeeded in flinging his assailant over, and then, faint from loss of blood, had missed his footing and fallen beside his dead antagonist. At any rate, when the corpse was discovered life had been extinct for several hours; and it was the opinion of the medical authorities who conducted the post-mortem that death was due not so much to the injuries themselves as to asphyxiation in the act of falling.

* * *

The jury found it "Death from accidental circumstances." Cleer never knew more than that her father had met his end by walking over the edge of a cliff on Dartmoor.

* * *

But when the body came home for burial, Dr. Yate-Westbury looked in by Mrs. Trevennack's special request, and performed an informal and private examination of the brain and nervous system. At the close of the autopsy he came down to the drawing-room where the silver-haired lady sat pale and tearful, but courageous. "It is just as I thought," he said; "a clot of blood, due to external injury, has pressed for years above the left frontal region, causing hallucinations and irregularities of a functional character only. You needn't have the slightest fear of its proving hereditary. It's as purely accidental as a sprain or a wound. Your daughter, Mrs. Le Neve, couldn't possibly suffer for it."

And neither Cleer nor Le Neve nor anyone else ever shared that secret of Trevennack's delusions with his wife and the doctor.

Choose from Thousands of 1stWorldLibrary Classics By

Adolphus WilliamWard
Aesop
Agatha Christie
Alexander Aaronsohn
Alexander Kielland
Alexandre Dumas
Alfred Gatty
Alfred Ollivant
Alice Duer Miller
Alice Turner Curtis
Alice Dunbar
Ambrose Bierce
Amelia E. Barr
Andrew Lang
Andrew McFarland Davis
Anna Sewell
Annie Besant
Annie Hamilton Donnell
Annie Payson Call
Anton Chekhov
Arnold Bennett
Arthur Conan Doyle
Arthur Ransome
Atticus
B. M. Bower
Basil King
Bayard Taylor
Ben Macomber
Booth Tarkington
Bram Stoker
C. Collodi
C. E. Orr
C. M. Ingleby
Carolyn Wells
Catherine Parr Traill
Charles A. Eastman
Charles Dickens
Charles Dudley Warner
Charles Farrar Browne
Charles Ives
Charles Kingsley
Charles Lathrop Pack
Charles Whibley
Charles Willing Beale
Charlotte M. Braeme
Charlotte M.Yonge
Clair W. Hayes
Clarence Day Jr.
Clarence E. Mulford

Clemence Housman
Confucius
Cornelis DeWitt Wilcox
Cyril Burleigh
D. H. Lawrence
Daniel Defoe
David Garnett
Don Carlos Janes
Donald Keyhole
Dorothy Kilner
Dougan Clark
E. Nesbit
E.P.Roe
E. Phillips Oppenheim
Edgar Allan Poe
Edgar Rice Burroughs
Edith Wharton
Edward J. O'Biren
John Cournos
Edwin L. Arnold
Eleanor Atkins
Elizabeth Cleghorn
Gaskell
Elizabeth Von Arnim
Ellem Key
Emily Dickinson
Erasmus W. Jones
Ernie Howard Pie
Ethel Turner
Ethel Watts Mumford
Eugenie Foa
Eugene Wood
Evelyn Everett-Green
Everard Cotes
F. J. Cross
Federick Austin Ogg
Ferdinand Ossendowski
Francis Bacon
Francis Darwin
Frances Hodgson Burnett
Frank Gee Patchin
Frank Harris
Frank Jewett Mather
Frank L. Packard
Frederick Trevor Hill
Frederick Winslow Taylor
Friedrich Kerst
Friedrich Nietzsche
Fyodor Dostoyevsky

Gabrielle E. Jackson
Garrett P. Serviss
Gaston Leroux
George Ade
Geroge Bernard Shaw
George Ebers
George Eliot
George MacDonald
George Orwell
George Tucker
George W. Cable
George Wharton James
Gertrude Atherton
Grace E. King
Grant Allen
Guillermo A. Sherwell
Gulielma Zollinger
Gustav Flaubert
H. A. Cody
H. B. Irving
H. G. Wells
H. H. Munro
H. Irving Hancock
H. Rider Haggard
H. W. C. Davis
Hamilton Wright Mabie
Hans Christian Andersen
Harold Avery
Harold McGrath
Harriet Beecher Stowe
Harry Houidini
Helent Hunt Jackson
Helen Nicolay
Hendy David Thoreau
Henrik Ibsen
Henry Adams
Henry Ford
Henry Frost
Henry James
Henry Jones Ford
Henry Seton Merriman
Henry Wadsworth
Longfellow
Henry W Longfellow
Herbert A. Giles
Herbert N. Casson
Herman Hesse
Homer
Honore De Balzac

Horace Walpole
Horatio Alger, Jr.
Howard Pyle
Howard R. Garis
Hugh Lofting
Hugh Walpole
Humphry Ward
Ian Maclaren
Israel Abrahams
J.G.Austin
J. Henri Fabre
J. M. Barrie
J. Macdonald Oxley
J. S. Knowles
J. Storer Clouston
Jack London
Jacob Abbott
James Allen
James Lane Allen
James Andrews
James Baldwin
James DeMille
James Joyce
James Oliver Curwood
James Oppenheim
James Otis
Jane Austen
Jens Peter Jacobsen
Jerome K. Jerome
John Burroughs
John F. Kennedy
John Gay
John Glasworthy
John Habberton
John Joy Bell
John Milton
John Philip Sousa
Jonathan Swift
Joseph Carey
Joseph Conrad
Joseph Jacobs
Julian Hawthrone
Julies Vernes
Justin Huntly McCarthy
Kakuzo Okakura
Kenneth Grahame
Kate Langley Bosher
L. A. Abbot
L. T. Meade
L. Frank Baum
Laura Lee Hope

Laurence Housman
Leo Tolstoy
Leonid Andreyev
Lewis Carroll
Lilian Bell
Lloyd Osbourne
Louis Tracy
Louisa May Alcott
Lucy Fitch Perkins
Lucy Maud Montgomery
Lydia Miller Middleton
Lyndon Orr
M. H. Adams
Margaret E. Sangster
Margaret Vandercook
Maria Edgeworth
Maria Thompson Daviess
Mariano Azuela
Marion Polk Angellotti
Mark Overton
Mark Twain
Mary Austin
Mary Cole
Mary Rowlandson
Mary Wollstonecraft
Shelley
Max Beerbohm
Myra Kelly
Nathaniel Hawthrone
O. F. Walton
Oscar Wilde
Owen Johnson
P.G.Wodehouse
Paul and Mable Thorn
Paul G. Tomlinson
Paul Severing
Peter B. Kyne
Plato
R. Derby Holmes
R. L. Stevenson
Rabindranath Tagore
Rahul Alvares
Ralph Waldo Emmerson
Rene Descartes
Rex E. Beach
Richard Harding Davis
Richard Jefferies
Robert Barr
Robert Frost
Robert Gordon Anderson
Robert L. Drake

Robert Lansing
Robert Michael Ballantyne
Robert W. Chambers
Rosa Nouchette Carey
Ross Kay
Rudyard Kipling
Samuel B. Allison
Samuel Hopkins Adams
Sarah Bernhardt
Selma Lagerlof
Sherwood Anderson
Sigmund Freud
Standish O'Grady
Stanley Weyman
Stella Benson
Stephen Crane
Stewart Edward White
Stijn Streuvels
Swami Abhedananda
Swami Parmananda
T. S. Ackland
The Princess Der Ling
Thomas A. Janvier
Thomas A Kempis
Thomas Anderton
Thomas Bailey Aldrich
Thomas Bulfinch
Thomas De Quincey
Thomas H. Huxley
Thomas Hardy
Thomas More
Thornton W. Burgess
U. S. Grant
Valentine Williams
Victor Appleton
Virginia Woolf
Walter Scott
Washington Irving
Wilbur Lawton
Wilkie Collins
Willa Cather
Willard F. Baker
William Makepeace
Thackeray
William W. Walter
Winston Churchill
Yei Theodora Ozaki
Young E. Allison
Zane Grey